"How can I get Tristan to notice me?"

"Tristan?" Alejandro stared at Jessica. "Tristan Patterson, our *TA?*" he asked.

"Normally I wouldn't need advice about letting a guy know I'm interested," J_____ explained, "But Tristan's _____ I don't want to co_____ with a crush."

What was _____uldn't suddenly give _____ ssica wasn't stupid, and he liked her too much to make himself happy at her expense.

"C'mon, Alejandro," Jessica prodded. "Help me out. You're a guy; you know how guys think."

Give her your really good idea, he told himself. *The guy's a TA; it's not like he'd make a move on a student in his class anyway.* There was probably some kind of policy against that. Alejandro relaxed—he didn't have to worry at all about Jessica and Tristan hooking up! She'd go for it, Patterson would rebuff her, and that would be the end of it!

And then Alejandro could ask her out. . . .

Bantam Books in the Sweet Valley University series.
Ask your bookseller for the books you have missed.

And don't miss these Sweet Valley
University Thriller Editions:

Visit the Official Sweet Valley Web Site on the Internet at:

http://www.sweetvalley.com

SWEET VALLEY UNIVERSITY®

Fooling Around

Written by
Laurie John

Created by
FRANCINE PASCAL

BANTAM BOOKS
NEW YORK · TORONTO · LONDON · SYDNEY · AUCKLAND

RL 8, age 14 and up

FOOLING AROUND
A Bantam Book / November 1999

Sweet Valley High® *and Sweet Valley University*®
are registered trademarks of Francine Pascal.
Conceived by Francine Pascal.

Produced by 17th Street Productions,
a division of Daniel Weiss Associates, Inc.
33 West 17th Street
New York, NY 10011.

ISBN: 0-553-49272-1

Published simultaneously in the United States and Canada

Bantam Books are published by Bantam Books, a division of Random
House, Inc. Its trademark, consisting of the words "Bantam Books" and
the portrayal of a rooster, is Registered in U.S. Patent and Trademark
Office and in other countries. Marca Registrada. Bantam Books, 1540
Broadway, New York, New York 10036.

PRINTED IN THE UNITED STATES OF AMERICA

OPM   0 9 8 7 6 5 4 3 2 1

To Molly Jessica W. Wenk

Chapter One

"He called me a bimbo!" Jessica Wakefield yelled, staring at Sam Burgess in disbelief. "What was I supposed to do, act like one and let him get away with it?"

She couldn't believe Sam's nerve—or that she was stuck living with him. For once Jessica wished she'd listened to Elizabeth. Her twin sister had been right when she'd insisted they'd regret letting Sam move in with them. "And calling Floyd a jughead wasn't exactly the nastiest thing I *could* have said, Sam." He stepped around her in the small kitchen to stand in front of the stove and flip his burning French toast.

Sam and his idiot friend Floyd had built a pyramid out of Sam's disgusting beer-can collection the day he'd moved into the duplex with Jessica, Elizabeth, and Neil Martin. The "sculpture" stood

1

in the living room, visible from any angle. Jessica, Elizabeth, and Neil had freaked—the fight had gone on all night.

Now, three days later, the stupid beer-can sculpture was still there, looking totally gross, but Floyd, thank God, had been banished from the duplex by Neil.

"Whatever," Sam said, forking his sizzling French toast onto a plate and drowning it in maple syrup. "I'm sick of arguing about it. The house rule is, everyone can invite over whoever they want, and everyone can put whatever stuff they want in the common rooms. If no one likes my friends or my beer-can collection, well, that's too bad." Leaning over the counter, he scarfed down his breakfast in four bites, then clunked the syrup-and-crumbs-coated plate in the sink. He downed the last of his coffee and set the mug on top of the plate, followed by the greasy pan and the spatula. "Nice chatting with you, Jess, but gotta go."

"At least the roaches we'll get from your un-washed dishes will have a duplex of their own—your beer-can sculpture!" Jessica poured another cup of coffee into her SVU mug and took a big gulp. She needed a ton of caffeine today. It was the second day of classes, and Jessica had a packed schedule.

Sam sent her a "you're-such-a-riot!" look, then stormed through the swinging doors just as Elizabeth was trying to push her way in. He muttered a "sorry," and then Jessica heard the front door slam.

Elizabeth rolled her eyes. "One of us having *another* argument with Sam? What a surprise," she deadpanned, opening the fridge to grab a yogurt. She plucked a spoon from the dish rack. "*Jessica!* You'd better be planning on washing your dishes."

"They're Sam's!" Jessica shrieked, annoyed that Elizabeth immediately assumed she'd be that inconsiderate. That was the *old* Jessica. *Hasn't anyone in this house noticed how much I've changed this past week alone? I'm practically a different person now that I'm a sophomore.*

Elizabeth rolled her eyes again and charged out of the kitchen—just as Neil was coming in. They definitely needed a system for that swinging door. Someone was going to get a smashed-in nose one of these days.

"What's with her?" Neil asked as he pulled open the fridge and poked around inside.

"Pissed at Sam, as usual," Jessica said. She glanced at her watch. "Ohmigod—it's almost ten! I'm gonna be late for art history! Today's the first discussion section." Jessica gulped the rest of her coffee, then dumped her mug on top of Sam's dishes in the sink. "It's your turn to wash, Neil, right?" she called over her shoulder as she dashed through the door.

*   *   *

"Cute-guy alert!"

Jessica glanced up from her art-history text-book. The girl sitting behind her in class was oohing and ahhing with her friend over some-one, but Jessica couldn't tell which guy. There were a few cute guys in the room, but no one worthy of a cute-guy alert, at least by Jessica's standards.

Whoa! she thought, catching sight of the Adonis who stood in front of the classroom. He was taking files out of a knapsack and stacking them on the professor's desk. *Cute* and/or *guy* didn't even begin to describe him. He was a *man*. At least twenty-two or twenty-three years old— and drop-dead gorgeous.

Was he the teaching assistant their professor, Dr. Devane, had mentioned would be leading their dis-cussion sections? Jessica hoped so. He was well worth waiting for, she thought, checking her watch. The TA had been five minutes late. She'd practically run to the arts building to make it on time, only to find everyone sitting around talking or doodling.

She was so grateful for the discussion sections, which were like mini go-over versions of the main class. She had the main class on Mondays and Wednesdays and the discussion sections on Tuesdays and Thursdays. When she'd walked into the lecture hall for the first main class yesterday,

4

she'd been shocked to see over a hundred students filling the auditorium. The discussion sections, though, were broken into groups of about twenty-five students and led by a graduate student.

The TA pulled more materials out of his knapsack, arranging them on the desk. *What great hair,* she thought, staring at him. Tousled, light brown, sort of longish . . . almost reaching his broad shoulders. From where she sat in the next-to-last row, Jessica couldn't tell what color his eyes were. Blue? Hazel? She had to know.

Jessica swept up her books, slung her knapsack over her shoulder, and darted into an empty seat in the third row. Just in time to see the TA's muscles bulge under his crisp oxford shirt as he took off his blazer.

"Jessica!" A cute Latino guy sitting one row up and one seat over had turned around and was smiling at her.

"Alejandro, how are you!" she exclaimed. She'd met Alejandro Morales, a freshman, in the financial-aid office last week, and he'd totally saved her butt. Jessica had found out from her adviser that she wasn't enrolled for the fall semester, and she'd run all over campus, from the registrar's to the bursar's to financial aid, trying to figure out what had happened and how to fix it. By the time she'd gotten to the front of the line at the right office, financial aid, the very nasty clerk had told her, "Sorry, it's five—we're closed," and Jessica had burst into tears.

Which, of course, had upset her even more. She was supposed to be a newly mature, newly serious sophomore, not a crybaby. Alejandro, who worked part-time in financial aid, took pity on her and discovered the computer glitch. She'd then bemoaned her next problem: having to declare a major. How was she supposed to choose from art history, English lit, fashion merchandising, psychology, and other interesting-sounding subjects when she had no idea what she wanted to do with her life? Alejandro had spoken so enthusiastically about his own choice for a major, art history, that Jessica had decided to declare it too. She'd taken a basic art-history class as a freshman and had liked it well enough, but last year she hadn't taken school very seriously. This year she was determined to change a lot of her ways—including becoming more studious.

"Move up here," he suggested, patting the empty desk next to his.

Jessica worked her way between the narrow row and settled into the seat next to him. "Thanks to you, here I am!" she told him. "I didn't see you yesterday in lecture—I can't believe how big that class is."

"I know—it was like sitting in assembly or something," he said. "I'm so psyched we're in the same discussion section—hey, what's *with* this TA,

6

though, huh? He's, like, ten minutes late, and now he's taking forever to get set up."

"None of the girls seem to mind just watching him," said a pretty girl sitting on the other side of Alejandro.

Jessica laughed. *You got that right, sister.*

"Jessica Wakefield, Chloe Murphy. Chloe Murphy, Jessica Wakefield," Alejandro introduced, leaning back so Jessica could shake the light-blue-nail-polished hand that extended across Alejandro's desk. "Chloe and I met at freshman orientation."

"Hi, Chloe," Jessica said with a smile. "I *totally* agree with you, by the way." *And at least I don't have to compete with you for our TA's attention,* she thought, feeling sort of bad about being catty. She was supposed to be more mature this year, but honestly, what was with Chloe's style? The girl had a really pretty face, striking ice blue eyes, and straight auburn hair, but she was a total fashion *don't*. She dressed like a guy—with baggy I-can't-even-figure-out-the-color cargo pants, a ratty gray T-shirt, and high-top black sneakers. The T-shirt wasn't even tucked in.

"Chloe missed the lecture class yesterday," Alejandro said. "So she's copying my notes."

Chloe leaned forward again. "I couldn't find the arts building—can you believe that? I feel like I'll never figure out this campus. Hey, do you think I could copy your notes too?" she asked

7

Jessica. "In case Alejandro missed something?"

"Mine?" Jessica was shocked. No one had ever asked to borrow her notes before. She couldn't remember ever having *taken* notes before—until yesterday, her first day of sophomore year. She passed her binder to Alejandro, who handed it to Chloe.

Chloe skimmed through Jessica's notes. "These are great! Lots better than yours, Alejandro."

Alejandro snatched his notebook from Chloe's desk. "I use my own special form of shorthand. Anyway, of course Jessica takes better notes— she's a sophomore."

"I knew it!" Chloe exclaimed, pushing a strand of red hair behind her ears. "I knew you couldn't be a freshman. You have that totally pulled-together look, like you know where you're going and what you're doing."

It was funny that Chloe should choose those words because that was exactly the feeling that had come over Jessica yesterday after the art-history lecture. As though she'd finally found her place and had a direction.

Chloe tapped her fingernails on Jessica's binder. "Is it okay if I take your notes so I can make a copy at the library? I'll return them tomorrow in lecture."

"Sure, go ahead," Jessica told her. "And don't

worry about getting lost around campus—you'll figure it out in a couple of weeks."

Chloe smiled. "I hope so," she said, removing the notes. She handed the binder back to Jessica. "Thanks for the notes—I really appreciate it. Now I know where to come when I need homework help. I'm pretty new to this art-history stuff."

Jessica was about to say that she was too. But she liked the way Chloe was looking up to her. Jessica hadn't been anyone's mentor since high school, if you counted hair and cheerleading as mentoring-worthy subjects. School, studying, and notes had always been Elizabeth's department.

"Good morning, everyone," boomed a sexy male voice from the front of the room. The TA smiled, eased back onto the edge of the desk, and scanned the room with amazing eyes that Jessica could now tell were dark blue. "I apologize for being so late—I do want our discussion group to be informal, but not *that* informal, so do as I say and not as I do—show up on time."

The girls in the class laughed, but Jessica could swear she saw Alejandro roll his eyes. *Someone* was jealous!

"I'm Tristan Patterson. I'd like to call you by your first names, so I invite you to do the same with me."

Tristan Patterson. The perfect name for a perfect-looking guy.

9

"As you know, this discussion group is an integral part of your art-history lecture class. We'll meet twice weekly, not only to examine the parts of text not covered in lectures, but also as a backup to understanding the lectures. Since there isn't always time for Dr. Devane to answer all your questions, that's my job. I want us to become a mutual-support group. I hope you all take the time to become acquainted with each other and me."

Oh, yes! I hope so too.

"Remember, I'm here to help you. So before we get started, I want you all to know where and when you can find me. I'm in office B-37. That's in the basement of this building. And I've written my office hours and telephone number on the board. Jot them down for future reference."

Jessica jotted.

He held up the humongous art-history book. "By now everyone should have managed to buy, borrow, or steal a copy of this very expensive and very heavy textbook." He flashed the warmest, sincerest, friendliest . . . sexiest smile Jessica had ever seen.

"Let's open to page twelve and start off today by comparing your text definition of *baroque* with Dr. Devane's definition, which I've written on the board."

But Jessica couldn't take her eyes off him. As he moved around the room, talking to the class, answering questions, sparking discussions, writing more words on the board, and pointing at pages in the textbook, Jessica could only stare at him.

Suddenly she realized she hadn't blinked in ten minutes. She glanced down at her notebook and winced. What would Chloe think of her superior sophomore intellect if she saw *these* notes? While Jessica had been staring at Call-me-Tristan, she had unconsciously doodled little hearts and flowers all over the page. Below Tristan's office hours and phone number were meaningless scrawls and squiggles.

She turned to a fresh page in her binder, glancing at Alejandro to see if he'd noticed, but he was too busy writing down every word Tristan was saying. It looked as if *she'd* be borrowing his notes this time.

Now, what was that definition of baroque? Jessica tried to find it on the board, but Tristan had erased that and moved on to something else. *Pay attention, Jessica!*

As he wrote something on the blackboard, she was once again mesmerized by the muscles working in his back . . . by his fingers as they held the chalk . . . by his chiseled profile . . . by the blondish highlights in his sexy, almost curly, almost longish hair. . . .

". . . and we also learned in yesterday's lecture that . . ."

Focus! she yelled at herself. Maybe TAs

11

shouldn't be this gorgeous. It was way too distracting.

"Chloe, over here!"

Ha! Chloe Murphy thought, dropping a fork and a napkin onto her tray. *Eva Bedford is waving me over to her lunch table! I've done it! Before last Friday, no one in my dorm even acknowledged my existence. And now I'm being sought out—by sophomores! Well, that's what having SVU's hunky quarterback for a boyfriend will do for a freshman.* Chloe wove her way to where Eva sat with Chloe's roommate, the vicious Moira Pierce, and several other girls from Oakley Hall.

Okay, pretend *boyfriend,* she amended. But if Chloe had her way, which it looked like she would, Tom Watts would be her *real* boyfriend any day now.

"Hi, everybody," she said, flashing her I'm-so-in-love-and-so-happy smile. Okay again, so she wasn't *in love* with Tom, but she did like him, and she'd probably fall in love with him once they started dating regularly. Tom was some kind of legend at SVU; he was the most amazing quarterback SVU had ever had.

The girls at the table smiled back, except of course for Moira. Moira was a sophomore and had made it clear she hated Chloe's guts on first sight.

Chloe took a bite of her cheeseburger. "I'm so

glad I didn't miss you guys for lunch—Tom called just as I was leaving the dorm, and he was telling me all about the surprise date he has planned for us tonight. He is so romantic!"

"You two make such a cute couple," Lisa Lewisi said. "You are *so* lucky."

Yeah—*lucky* that she'd actually gotten Tom Watts to ask her out on a real date for last Friday. When Tom had picked up Chloe, she had made sure that everyone was around to witness it. Especially Moira.

"I know," Chloe said between mouthfuls. "You wouldn't expect SVU's star quarterback to be so sweet and sensitive, but Tom is just amazing."

"Wow, so you probably go to all those really cool parties and know everybody!" one of the freshman girls said. "You must have the best social life!"

"You guys are gonna make me blush!" Chloe said in her most humble voice. What was *really* humbling was how pathetic she felt every time she spent five hours sitting alone in a diner far off campus—when everyone thought she was on a date with Tom. *How many more cups of coffee and fattening Danishes can I consume?*

"Where's Tom been picking you up lately?" Moira trained those cold, catlike green eyes on Chloe. "I haven't seen him around Oakley. Not once since last Friday."

"Um, well, I've been meeting him for our dates at other places," Chloe said, thinking fast. "We've been hanging out with mutual friends a lot. Like last night, we had dinner and drinks with Lila Fowler— she's a sophomore and *very* involved in Theta. She's the one who fixed us up on the blind date last spring, so we wanted to treat her to a really nice dinner. We had such a blast, and then we went to—"

"Oh my God!" a sophomore cut in. "Your boyfriend is the quarterback *and* you have a friend in Theta? Can you rub off on me, please?" The girl laughed.

Chloe beamed. *At least the blind-date story is true,* she thought, hoping her nose wouldn't grow *too* long from all her lying. Lila, a family friend who Chloe hadn't seen once since she arrived on campus, *had* set up Chloe with Tom last spring. She and Tom had had a good time, even sharing an amazing kiss, but she'd never heard from him again. She hadn't given him a moment's thought either—until she'd arrived at SVU and needed a name for the boyfriend she'd gushed about. Tom Watts had been the first name to come to mind, and boy, had she chosen well!

Suddenly she'd gone from being ignored to being sought out for advice, trips to the caf, boy talk, everything. Granted, none of the girls had become a best friend or anything, but at least she felt included, like she fit in.

Keeping up the lie was worth it. But since it meant producing Tom in the flesh at least once for credibility, Chloe had hung out in front of his dorm until she ran into him. And all she'd had to do after the "Tom-is-that-you?" speech was to pour on the "I'm just a freshman who doesn't know my way around campus," and suddenly they had a date.

But four days later, he hadn't called for a second date . . . hadn't returned any of her phone calls either. And unless Chloe could make him her real boyfriend fast, her I-notice-everything roommate—who was staring at Chloe with that I-hate-your-guts look—was going to get suspicious.

Dana Upshaw dumped the macaroni from the box into the pot of boiling water, jumping back to keep from getting splashed. She was wearing the fuzzy, cropped black sweater that Todd loved, and she didn't want it to smell like macaroni. Not that macaroni smelled like anything, Dana realized, sniffing over the pot. Was that because it was from a box?

Anyway, even if it was just mac and cheese, she felt like a real adult as she made a hot lunch for her and Todd. She'd gone to classes all morning, then had rushed home, undone the topknot her hair had been in, whisked on a little lipstick, changed into something sexy, and started cooking. Exactly like she imagined married career women

15

did. She and Todd weren't married, of course, but they did live together. If she didn't have school, she could accomplish so much more, she thought, stirring the pasta. The apartment would be spotless and the fridge packed, and she'd have time to think of fun things for her and Todd to do at night now that they lived so far off campus.

She set the small, round table, which was just plastic but looked great covered with the lavender tablecloth she'd bought cheap at a flea market. Wineglasses, a white candle, and daisies blooming in a little vase made the table look so elegant, she thought, admiring how Martha Stewart she was becoming.

Dana glanced at her watch. Todd would be home in about five minutes. She'd timed everything perfectly, which, if she said so herself, she'd managed to accomplish every day since she and Todd moved in together—a whole week now. She gave the macaroni a good stir, then dashed downstairs to get the mail.

The apartment building's lobby was kind of dingy, but Dana loved the brass mailbox that had both of their names on it. Todd Wilkins, Dana Upshaw. A fact nobody could dispute. Somehow it made their living arrangement seem more official. She ran her fingers over the nameplate. Someday, maybe in the not-too-distant future, it would say

Todd and Dana Wilkins. Humming a melody that she should have been practicing on her cello, Dana grabbed the stack of mail and thumbed through it on her way back upstairs. By the time she reached the second floor, she stopped humming. The mail was all bills: telephone, gas, electricity, and cable. *How could we have bills already?* she wondered. They'd just moved in a week ago! She ripped open the envelopes and saw that the utilities charged for the *coming* month, not the previous one. Oh.

She sighed. It had been hard enough to scavenge up enough money for everything when she'd had four roommates. Now with just her and Todd, it seemed impossible—especially since neither of them had a job. Todd refused to use the cushy bank account his parents had given him for anything other than tuition; he wanted to use his *own* money to take care of his and Dana's new life together. That was sweet and noble and all that, but Todd didn't have much money of his own, and neither did she. It wasn't like he was living in the dorms anymore and eating on a prepaid meal plan. Suddenly tuition didn't include rent, food, and utilities. But Todd was adamant. So what were they going to do?

She pushed open the apartment door and was hit by a burning smell and a sizzling noise. *The macaroni!* As she sprinted to the stove, she dropped the mail on the table and accidentally elbowed a wineglass, which crashed to the floor. Cursing, she turned off the burner, then grabbed a dishrag to move the pot to the counter. The water had boiled out, leaving the pasta glued to itself and to the bottom of the pan.

Dana almost burst into tears. Lunch was ruined. And now she'd have to spend an hour scraping clean the bottom of the stupid pot, the only one they had. She looked over at the pieces of broken glass littering the floor, and suddenly it was too much. Reality. Macaroni and cheese from a sixtynine-cent box, a stack of bills, and one wineglass.

Tears stinging the backs of her eyes, Dana used the edge of the macaroni box for a dustpan and scooped up the glass. As she dumped it in the garbage can, all she could think about was how pathetic things really were. She wasn't a married career woman. She was a sophomore in college who lived with her boyfriend in the only apartment they could afford—a tiny dump forty minutes' walk from campus. Relying on her junky used car to get to school was a joke, and her cello barely fit in the back. Yesterday, the first day of classes, she'd spent ten minutes trying to get her cello out of the car in the campus's commuter parking lot. And then she'd been late for her cello seminar, which affected her playing.

Worse, today she'd been so conscious of how embarrassed she'd been yesterday that she'd played badly again.

The whole apartment reeked of burned food. Dana opened the windows in the living room and in the tiny bedroom, then slumped onto the sofa and flung her hands over her face. It wasn't supposed to be like this.

"Dana?" Todd called from the doorway. "What's going on? Why's the door wide open? What's that smell?"

Todd. Thank God. She sat up and held out her arms to him. She just needed a hug, then she'd be fine.

"*Dana,* something's burning," he said, staring at her like she was a martian as he hurried past her into the kitchen. Dana's arms slumped down to her sides, and she followed him.

He picked up a wooden spoon and poked it into the pot. "Okay, *not* burning. *Burned,*" he amended. He looked at her and seemed to realize she'd been crying. "Dana? Is this why you're so upset? It's no big deal. It'll be fine once we add the milk and the cheese packet."

"It's totally ruined, Todd," she said. "And that was the last box. I could make us tuna fish if you want."

He opened the fridge and grabbed the milk,

pouring some into the pot. Then he ripped open the cheese packet and dumped it in.

"Look—it's fine," he said, tipping the pot to show her as he stirred hard. "Just a little charred."

He ladled out two portions into bowls, stuck a fork in each, and brought them to the table. He sat down and looked up at her with the sweetest expression on his face, as if he were in a palace and had perfectly cooked filet mignon or swordfish in front of him.

Why didn't he care? Dana wondered as she sat down across from him. Why didn't this bother him? She didn't get it.

"There's no way you're this upset about the macaroni getting a little scorched," Todd said between giant mouthfuls. "Something's up. Spill it."

"I don't know," she told him, pushing her pasta around. "It's like a combination of things, you know? I didn't have the greatest day at school, and then I screwed up lunch, and we got all these bills. Maybe we should cancel cable, Todd."

"No way," he replied. "I'm not giving up ESPN. Cable's not that expensive." He got up and disappeared into the kitchen, returning with the carton of milk. He filled his wineglass. "We'll work everything out. Last week neither of us even had a place to live, and here we are, in our own apartment. Don't worry, okay?"

20

Dana breathed a sigh of relief. "You're figuring we've always got the bank account if we get desperate, right?" she asked.

He stared at her. "*No*, I'm not figuring that at all. You know how I feel about using that money, Dana. I want to take care of us *myself*. I'll just get a job."

"But if you get a job, between work and school we'd *never* see each other," Dana complained. "I think you should just forget your pride and use the money. It's for paying your way through school, which is where you *are*."

"That money is for tuition and books," he snapped. "My parents have no idea I'm living off campus *or* with my girlfriend. And I'm not going to take care of you by sponging off them. You can't understand that?"

She slouched in her chair and twisted her napkin in her hands. "Todd, I do understand it—I really do. It's incredible of you to want to be responsible for us. But be realistic, okay? That's all I'm saying."

"I said I'd get a job, and you tell me not to. Now you're telling *me* to be realistic? *Let's live like adults, Todd, but on your parents' money 'cause you can't take care of us.*' That's what you're saying, Dana." Todd pushed aside his bowl and dropped his fork in it, his frustration evident. "Look, I have to go—I need to buy my economics textbook before the class this afternoon." Todd scraped back his chair and got up.

"Todd, come on," Dana said. "You're just gonna walk out? That's how adult *you* are?"

That was the wrong thing to say, she realized. Todd slammed out the door. *Great.* Now she'd depressed him *and* pissed him off. She *did* trust him. But wasn't he being totally naive?

What happened to the way things were? she wondered, staring at the burned edge of a macaroni. Just last week they'd been unable to keep their hands off each other, fixing up their tiny apartment, so happy to be living together. And now they were barely getting along. What was so terrible about using his parents' money? Dana didn't get it. If she had access to that kind of money, they'd be living in major style. Without that money they couldn't live like adults, like a real couple—the way Todd wanted them to live. Didn't he understand that? And didn't he understand that a job wasn't the answer?

"Living off campus is so amazing, Nina. The freedom is great—totally worth the responsibility of having your own place." Elizabeth Wakefield pressed the phone receiver more tightly against her ear and stuck a finger in her other ear. "Nina, I'm going to have to call you back," she shouted. "Sam's stereo is so loud downstairs, I can't even hear myself."

"I said, I can't talk now anyway," Nina shouted back. "Bye," she added, and hung up.

Elizabeth hung up too, stung by Nina's attitude. Her best friend was doing it again, Elizabeth realized. Shutting her out. Elizabeth knew that Nina was getting over a broken heart, but hadn't they resolved just last week to reach out to each other in times of crisis? To support each other like best friends were supposed to?

"Wakefield!" Sam screeched from the bottom of the stairs. "Hey, Elizabeth!"

Elizabeth scrambled off her bed and walked into the hallway. *"What?"* she called down the stairs.

He yelled back something, but she couldn't hear him over the pounding music. Her attic room was on the third floor, and Sam's was on the first. But he had this irritating habit of blasting his stereo and keeping his door open. "Sam! Turn down your stereo!" she yelled. She waited. No response. Music still blared.

Seething, she stomped down the two flights to find Sam sprawled across the living-room floor, right next to his precious beer-can pyramid. The sight of that thing still made Elizabeth's stomach churn.

"Sam!" Elizabeth shouted.

It wasn't the stereo in his room that was blasting—it was the boom box they kept on the living room's window seat. She marched over to it and turned the volume way down.

Sam finally noticed her presence. "Oh, good—you're off the phone," he said, sitting up. A huge textbook lay next to him, and a sandwich wrapped in foil and a giant-sized bag of pretzels were on top of it.

"*That's* what you wanted?" she asked through gritted teeth. Sam was so selfish and immature. "Why didn't you just pick up the receiver to see if I was off instead of screeching at me when I was *on?*"

"Because then you'd go ballistic on me for listening in on your conversation." He lay back down, his hands intertwined behind his head. His black T-shirt rode up a bit, and Elizabeth could see his belly button. How a guy who did nothing all day—except lie around listening to music or playing video games—managed to have rock-solid abs was beyond her. "Can you hand me the phone?" he asked, gesturing at the cordless near the boom box.

"Sam, get something straight," she snarled. "I'm not your personal servant. That also means I—or Jess or Neil—don't wash your dishes either. And the next time you use *my* milk, be nice enough to put it back in the refrigerator. Got it?"

"If I'd known it was skim before I doused my cereal in it, I wouldn't even have used it," he announced with a smirk.

Elizabeth wanted to strangle that smirk off his incredibly good-looking face. What a total jerk he was!

She headed into the kitchen to make herself a

bowl of cereal, but the container of milk she'd just bought yesterday was now empty—and still in the fridge, of course. She was going to *kill* him.

Sam Burgess had driven her crazy all summer while they'd competed in a televised road-trip challenge. One minute she'd be yelling at him and the next minute she'd be kissing him, *real* kisses, *long* kisses. *Amazing* kisses. But Sam wasn't responsible enough to throw away a carton of empty milk, let alone build a relationship. She'd found that out fast. The summer hadn't been a total bust, though—she and Jessica had met Neil too, and he was such a great housemate that he almost made up for Sam.

She dumped the carton in the trash and rooted around the fridge for the peanut-butter-and-jelly sandwich she'd made for yesterday's lunch but hadn't eaten. *Where is it? I put it right here.* Sam!

She marched back into the living room just in time to see Sam taking a bite of her sandwich and licking a drop of grape jelly off his lip.

That's it, she told herself. *This is war.*

Chapter
Two

"Want another?" Alejandro asked as Jessica slurped the last of her cappuccino. *Please say yes*, he prayed silently. He needed more time to work up the nerve to ask her out—on a real date. That she'd accepted his invitation to join him for coffee after their art-history discussion section was a good indication that he had a chance.

"Definitely," she said. "I'll need the caffeine to keep me up later. Do you believe all the reading we've been assigned already?" She set her tall mug on the little round table and licked a bit of froth from her upper lip. "Ooh, and I want whatever that is," she exclaimed, pointing at something that looked like a brownie on a passing waitress's tray.

Alejandro signaled their waitress and gave their order. That brownie was so big, it would take her at least a half hour to finish it. That meant he had thirty minutes to cough up the guts to ask her out.

"You know, Alejandro? I'm not even freaking about our art-history homework—I'm actually into it. I can't believe it, *me*, psyched about doing homework! Yesterday's lecture and today's discussion—it's all so fascinating. I really owe you big time for steering me in the right direction."

The waitress delivered their second round, and Jessica split the brownie in two and pushed half toward him on a napkin. "So, do you know what you want to do with your art degree?" she asked, taking a bite and closing her eyes as she savored it.

"I'm thinking art preservation," he told her, picking a walnut piece out of the brownie and popping it in his mouth. "Last year I read about this man who restored masterpieces, and I got really psyched and started reading everything I could find about the subject."

"You're so lucky you're so directed," she said. "You saw what a panic I was in last week about having to declare a major. Picture me trying to decide about a career!"

She certainly was praising him a lot, Alejandro noticed. Did that mean she liked him? She was smiling at him, and every now and then she'd briefly touch his arm. That meant something, right?

"But you know what's so cool?" she continued.

"I had no idea a person could consider so many careers just from one major! I guess I figured if you major in art history, you become an art historian. Isn't that so stupid?"

"It's not stupid at all, Jess," he responded. "That's what college is all about. You discover new stuff that you never even heard about before. You get to figure out what interests you, what you like, what bores you."

"I'm beginning to appreciate that," she said. "Last year I didn't take school very seriously, but now I'm really into all the opportunities. Hey, do you think I could run an art gallery one day? That sounds amazing."

Alejandro thought Jessica could probably fly if she wanted to. "You'd be great. You're really social, so all you need is the background knowledge."

"Which I'm getting, thanks to your help." Jessica touched his arm and smiled.

He couldn't take his eyes off her hand, where it rested just above his wrist. Her pale fingers contrasted against his darker skin. *This must mean she's interested, right? Would she actually say yes if I asked her out?* he wondered. *I'm just a freshman, though. No way.* But she *was* flirting, he realized. Smiling, laughing, praising him, *touching* him.

Ask her out, he told himself. *Do it. What have you got to lose . . . aside from your dignity if she says no?* He opened his mouth, but all that came out was, "Wanna split another brownie?"

"Oh, no, thanks—I couldn't eat another bite." She patted her tummy. "Alejandro," she said slowly. "Can I ask you something?"

Ohmigod, he thought. She was going to ask him out! Here he was, freaking about whether to ask *her* out, and the whole time she'd been planning to ask him!

"It's sort of personal—about dating," she continued.

Alejandro leaned forward eagerly.

"Well . . . do you think age differences matter in relationships?" she asked.

Definitely not! he wanted to shout. "I don't see how a year or two in either direction matters. You know, like a junior or a sophomore girl dating a freshman guy or something."

Her beaming smile told him she liked his answer. "Or the other way around," she said.

"Sure, yeah. Attraction is attraction, right?" Alejandro smiled. *It's now or never,* he thought. *She's clearly dropping the hint.* He cleared his throat and scooted his chair a little closer to her side of the table. He was close enough to smell her perfume.

"I am so glad to hear you say that, Alejandro," Jessica whispered. "I really need a guy's perspective on this, and you've given me such great advice."

She looked around, as if she didn't want anyone to hear her. "Okay, so now that we both agree age shouldn't be an issue, what do you think is the best way to get Tristan to notice me?"

"*Tristan?*" Alejandro nearly choked on his coffee. He could feel his cheeks turning red. He'd been saved from opening his big mouth and making a total idiot of himself, but now he felt sick to his stomach. "Tristan Patterson, our *TA?*" he asked when he'd recovered his voice

"Normally I wouldn't need advice about letting a guy know I'm interested, but Tristan's older— he's a grad student. I don't want to come across as some silly undergrad with a crush."

"I'm sure he'll notice you in class, if he hasn't already," Alejandro pointed out as nonchalantly as he could.

"Maybe," she said with a slight frown. "But there are like twenty-five people in our discussion section, and I'm sure we're not his only class. I can't just wait around and *hope* he'll notice me—I need to *make* him notice me."

Exactly why I like you so much, Alejandro thought. *You go for what you want.* What was he supposed to say? He couldn't suddenly give her *bad* advice—Jessica wasn't stupid, and he liked her too much to make himself happy at her expense.

"C'mon, Alejandro. Help me out. You're a

guy; you know how guys think." She laid her hand on top of his. But this time he recognized it for what it was—a *friendly* gesture.

Alejandro gulped his espresso. "I'd say, um, a *conservative* approach is the way to go. You know, because he's a grad student. If he were a frat pledge, all you'd have to do is walk past him in a tight shirt and he'd be yours."

Jessica laughed and leaned toward him, rapt with interest.

"Why don't you tell him you need help with the next assignment?" Alejandro suggested. "After the Thursday's discussion session." He hoped she'd jump on this just-okay suggestion. He didn't want to offer up the really good one—the one that was sure to get her what she wanted.

Jessica tilted her head to one side and gnawed at her bottom lip. She was considering it, he saw. She didn't look thrilled. *Damn. I like you so much, I don't want you to go out with him. But I like you so much, I want to see you happy too.*

"I don't know," she said. "I mean, it's a good idea, but he might tell me to just read the chapters and to catch him next time if I still have questions."

Give her your really good idea, he told himself. *The guy's a TA; it's not like he'd make a move on a student anyway. Not one in his own discussion section. Wow,* Alejandro thought, *that's right.* There was probably some kind of policy against that. Alejandro didn't have to worry at all about Jessica and Tristan hooking up! She'd go for it, he'd rebuff her, and that would be the end of it! And then Alejandro could ask her out.

"Tell him you need extra help and ask him if he has time for a tutoring session, just to go over the first week's classes." Alejandro relaxed back in his chair.

"Tutoring! *Brilliant,*" she exclaimed. "Why didn't I think of that?" She shot up from her seat and gave Alejandro a quick hug. "Thanks, Alejandro. I'm going straight to his office right now!"

Right now? She must really like this guy, he thought dejectedly, watching her skip out the door with a determined smile. Alejandro tried to hope she'd be over Tristan Patterson by the end of the week—maybe in time for Alejandro to ask her to a movie Saturday night.

Where the hell am I? Todd wondered, looking around at the unfamiliar intersection.

Great. Now I'm lost. He'd been so pissed off at Dana that he'd stormed out of the apartment and walked hard and fast without paying attention to where he was going. At least the walk had cleared his head. But now, instead of feeling angry and frustrated, he felt bad.

He was the one who'd made all this happen,

the one who'd decided he and Dana should live together, the one who'd found the place, signed the lease, and brought Dana there with a "ta-da!" And now that she was worried about money to pay for it, he was getting all mad at her. That wasn't fair. And it wasn't fair that he hadn't thought about *how* they were going to afford to live when he'd signed the lease. All he'd cared about was being with her.

Maybe I should just use that bank account—to make things nicer for Dana, he thought. *But how am I supposed to look at myself in the mirror if I'm using my father's money to take care of my girlfriend?*

Todd stared up at the sky and sighed. *Ah,* he thought, seeing one of SVU's tall dorms looming in the distance. He was between home and campus, so he wasn't that lost. He'd figured he'd come at least three or four miles from the apartment.

A skinny brown cat suddenly appeared next to him and rubbed against his calf. He squatted down to scratch the ugly thing behind the ears and to retie his shoelace—and that's when he noticed a large orange footprint painted on the sidewalk. And another a few feet up. And another. A whole row of them.

He straightened up and followed the footprints down the block, where he saw a colorful awning on the corner. *Frankie's* was spelled out in a funky script in different-colored letters across the bright red awning.

Frankie's. Why is that familiar? he wondered, then remembered. A couple of days ago he'd been getting the mail when he heard two young women talking about how psyched they were that Frankie's opened last weekend. They were complaining that unless you wanted to hang out with frat boys from SVU or old men in dive bars, there was nowhere nice to go to drink and dance. Frankie's was supposed to be the solution.

Curious, he peeked through the window on the side of the bar, but a handmade help-wanted sign caught his attention. Was this an omen or what?

Todd ran a hand through his wavy hair, wiped the sweat from his forehead, and pushed open the door. He blinked, waiting for his eyes to adjust to the club's dark interior.

Wow, he thought, looking around the room. The place was cool! The walls were sponge painted a pale yellow, and there were a lot of two- and four-person wood tables painted different colors, which circled around a space he assumed was the dance floor. A wrought-iron candlestick was on every table.

A long bar stretched across the entire left side, with stools that each had a letter painted on them spelling out Frankie's . . . twice, he counted. Huge abstract paintings were all over the walls.

Along the far back wall were two overstuffed sofas, a pool table, and a dartboard. Todd saw a small DJ booth, and there was a jukebox too. This place was amazing! He could just imagine what it would look like with the lights on and people hanging out.

"Hello?" Todd called out. His voice echoed in the empty room. "Is anyone here?"

A pretty redhead popped up from behind the bar. She had a bunch of limes in each hand. "We're not open for another four hours—6 P.M.," she informed him.

"Uh, no, I'm here about the job?" Todd said, pointing at the sign in the window.

"Oh, well, then give me just a sec," she replied. "Have a seat," she added, disappearing under the bar again.

Todd sat on a stool with a red N on it. He couldn't get over how great this place was. He could see why the women in his building were so excited—Frankie's was swanky. The bars he usually went to were just big or small rooms with ugly old tables and rowdy-student-proofed furniture.

The woman popped up again and wiped her hands on a bar towel. She smiled at Todd. "Rita," she said, holding out her hand. "I'm the manager."

"Todd Wilkins," he told her, shaking her hand. He liked her instantly. She was in her early thirties,

Todd figured. She had warm brown eyes and long, curly red hair. A few freckles across her nose and cheeks. She was really attractive. And she looked like the kind of woman you didn't mess with.

"College guy, right?" she said.

He nodded.

"Do you have experience working in a bar or club?" she asked.

"Uh, no . . . but I really need a job," he told her. "I just moved into a new apartment and—"

"Nearby? Or on campus?" she asked.

"Just a few miles from here—Lincoln Avenue," he replied.

"That's not exactly the high-rent district," she pointed out.

No kidding, he thought. "High enough for me to need a job," he told her.

She looked him over. "You're not twenty-one yet, are you?"

Todd considered lying but doubted that she'd believe him anyway. He shook his head.

"Can't use you as relief for Cathy, then," she said. "Cathy's the bartender, and I help her out when it gets busy."

"Listen, I'll do whatever," Todd said, trying to keep the pleading note out of his voice. "I'll wash dishes, wipe tables, mop floors, be a bouncer—"

"Can you work weekends?" she asked.

"Weekends, weekdays . . . You name it." *Please, please, please,* Todd prayed.

She pursed her lips and looked him over again. "Okay, then. I have a good feeling about you. You're hired."

Yes! Todd hopped off the bar stool and extended his hand toward her. She shook it, smiling at him. "Thank you *so* much," he told Rita. "You won't regret this, I promise."

"I like your enthusiasm, kid," she said. "You're our new bar back."

"What does a bar back do?" he asked.

"Everything you said you'd do to get the job. Basically you're helping me and Cathy, and Monica and Annie, the waitresses—you make sure there are always glasses for the bar, you collect empty glasses from the tables, keep the bar cleaned off, empty ashtrays, slice lemons, whatever. . . . It only pays minimum wage, but just make yourself indispensable, and you'll go far. Can you start tomorrow night?"

"Yes!" Todd exclaimed. He couldn't believe how perfect this was.

"Your shift starts at 6 P.M., but get here about twenty minutes early tomorrow so we can fill out your forms—paperwork, social security numbers, and all that boring stuff. After we close up tomorrow, we can work out your schedule."

"I'll be here," Todd said. "Thank you again."

She smiled, then disappeared under the bar. Todd took a last look at his new place of employment and walked out. He noticed the skinny cat lapping up food in a little dish on the curb. A bowl of water was next to it. *Probably Rita's doing,* he realized. *Caring woman.*

He had a job. And not just some loser job at a fast-food place or stocking shelves in a supermarket. Best of all, he could take care of Dana on *his* terms. All their problems were solved.

Dana pushed her way through the students hanging out in front of the music building. Despite the fact that she was loaded down like a pack camel, no one bothered to open the door for her. She slipped in behind someone else who was entering, but she wasn't quick enough. She caught the door with her hip and yelped as her heavy cello case banged against her shin for the hundredth time since leaving the parking lot. This afternoon she'd been smart enough to arrive ten minutes early for her first mixed-strings class, knowing she'd need the time to get her stupid cello out of the car. Of course, no one had offered to help her as she'd struggled with it.

She should just rent a locker, she thought. But that took money. . . . At the end of the hallway the elevator doors started closing. "Hold the elevator, please!" she shouted.

A hand shot out at the last second and caught the doors. "Can you hurry up?" a girl called out. "I'm gonna be late."

Bitch, Dana thought, stepping in and propping her cello case against the wall. She readjusted her armful of music, notebooks, and books. The jerk in the elevator was carrying a violin case and one sheet of music. The elevator thunked to a stop on the third floor, and the girl sauntered out.

Dana gave her cello case a kick to get it moving and hoisted it again, trying to get out the doors before they shut on her.

When she reached the practice hall, she lurched her way over to the front-row seat she'd occupied last year. She thought about taking a seat in the back. This year she had Professor Prichard, the new head of the department. Not only was he the toughest professor around, but he'd never heard her play before. She'd have to prove herself all over again. *Don't be an idiot,* she instantly yelled at herself. *You're good. All you have to do is concentrate and play.*

As she dropped into her seat, she heaved a tired sigh.

"Are you okay?" asked the girl next to her.

Dana looked at the girl. She was tall and thin, with long, glossy black hair nearly to her waist and eyes so dark black, they glittered. Her cello was against her shoulder and her bow poised to play—already.

"I'm Becky." The girl laid her bow across her lap and held out her hand.

Dana shook it. "Dana."

"Hey, Beck," a girl sitting behind them interrupted. "Do you know what piece we're starting with?"

"No, but I hope it's the Vivaldi concerto. I practiced that for two hours yesterday."

"Me too," a third girl added. "I was up till midnight. I would have practiced longer, but my roommate told me if I played another note, she was going to break my violin over my head."

"Anytime you guys need a place to practice, you should come over to my house," Becky offered. "My parents turned our garage into a studio for me. Acoustic walls and everything. They said, 'Honey, we love you, but six hours a day is too much for anyone to take.'"

Six hours? Get a life! Dana thought.

"Are you a freshman too?" Becky asked Dana.

"No, I'm a sophomore," Dana replied, wondering how a freshman had become so friendly with people already.

"Oh, cool." Becky waited for Dana to say something else, but Dana didn't feel like making small talk. She bent over and busied herself with

41

opening her cello case. *What's my problem?* she wondered. *Why am I being so bitchy?*

But she knew why. It was because she didn't really want to be here. She had hoped Todd might come back after storming out, but he hadn't. And since the tension between them was left unresolved, it would affect her playing, Dana knew. Again.

Plus she'd planned to clean the bathroom before leaving for campus, but she hadn't gotten to it because it had taken her an hour to scrub clean that stupid pot. She needed the pot for tonight, for the special dinner she was planning to make for Todd—to make up for today's lunch and their fight. Now the bathroom was still a mess, her playing arm was aching from scrubbing anyway, and Todd was still mad at her.

Dana looked around the studio. Everyone seemed so intense, so eager-faced, discussing sonatas and concertos and practice as if there was nothing else to talk about. She bet that none of these people had their own apartment and paid their own bills. They all probably lived in the dorms or at home and had every creature comfort. Of course *they* could practice for hours a day.

The professor walked in and rapped his baton against his music stand. Dana grappled her cello into position. "Good morning, students." Even standing on a foot-high riser, Professor Prichard was a short little man, but with a booming, curt voice. "I'd like you all to briefly introduce yourself with a piece. We'll start with the violins. Two-octave scale, ascending and descending, then the first ten bars of Rachmaninoff's Sonata in G Minor. Young man, you first." He pointed his baton at a guy in the front row.

The violinist was good. Really good. And so was the next girl . . . and the next and the next. Everyone in the first row was good except Becky, who was remarkable. Dana listened openmouthed as Becky coaxed a string of flawless notes from her cello. Even her scales were played with passion.

It was Dana's turn. Suddenly her left hand cramped and her shoulder stiffened. Her fingers refused to press the correct strings. And her bow felt as heavy as the pot of leftover macaroni and cheese. Somehow she managed to stumble through her scales, but reading the music proved even harder. Not only had she neglected to look over the familiar sonata this past week; she couldn't even do a decent cold reading. She finished the world's worst performance and heaved a sigh of relief, but she couldn't look up.

She could feel everyone staring at her, mocking her. She knew what Becky must be thinking: *This is the best you can do, and you're a* sophomore?

Dana felt hot and dizzy. Both rows behind her

finished their intros before her hands stopped trembling and she could breathe normally.

The professor rapped against his music stand, then raised his baton. "Let's start with one of the shorter pieces. Page thirty-two, Bartók's Rhapsody No.1."

Dana flipped her pages. . . . *Please be here. Please don't let me have forgotten to bring that piece.* Finding the music, she relaxed a little and began grinding out notes. At least with everyone else playing, she didn't sound so obviously unprepared.

"No. No. No." Professor Prichard's belly shook as he bounced onto his toes and waved them to a halt. "What am I hearing?" He poked a stubby finger into his ear and wriggled it back and forth. "Do I hear a screeching cat? Focus, people! Let it flow." He waved his hands in front of his chest to illustrate the concept of smooth.

Although he didn't even glance in her direction, Dana was certain that he was talking directly to her. She tensed her fingers against the frets and tried harder. This was awful! Even when she hit the right notes, which wasn't often, her playing was expressionless and as flat as "Jingle Bells" played by one of those high-pitched musical Christmas cards.

Again the professor rapped for attention, stopped them, scolded them, and started them up again.

Dana felt sick. Since eighth grade the cello had been her whole world. Her talent was her life. What had happened?

The other students' music drowned out her mistakes, but Dana felt each and every one. Her timing was completely off. It was her own fault—she hadn't been practicing lately. But practicing seemed like a luxury she couldn't afford this past week—she had an apartment to settle into and a live-in boyfriend to adjust to.

Maybe I'd be better off just faking it. I'll let the others carry me for a while. But pantomiming was harder than really playing. Distracted by the effort of trying *not* to play, Dana lost her place completely. She sat for a full minute, her bow poised in the air, frantically scanning the pages of music in front of her.

She saw Becky reach out to turn the page, so Dana reached out to flip her own. Several pages of her music fell from the stand and flittered to the floor. Her face burning, she slid from her chair and gathered the pages. The professor stopped them again.

Dana cringed, waiting for his booming voice to tell her to hurry it up. When it didn't, she slapped her music back on the stand and slipped back into her seat.

She glanced up and as she feared, every eye in

45

the room was turned toward her—including Professor Prichard's. Once a lover of the spotlight, she wanted nothing more at that moment than to be invisible.

"Are we ready now?" he asked in a quiet but sarcastic tone.

"Yes, sir. Sorry." Dana raised her bow. But she was far from ready. Her pages were in total disarray.

As the class began to play, Becky's foot snaked out and tapped Dana on the ankle. Then without the slightest facial expression and without missing a note, Becky used her foot to scoot her music stand close enough for Dana to read.

Dana tried again to jump back into the music, but even with Becky's perfectly arranged score in front of her she still had trouble. It was hard to read through her teary vision—she didn't know whether Becky's gesture was out of kindness or pity.

The class finally ended. Dana snapped her case shut and hurried straight to the bathroom. She had exactly thirty minutes to fix her tear-streaked makeup and get calmed down enough to cope with English lit.

She was standing in front of the sink, dabbing her eyes with paper towels, when Becky and several people from her class entered. They had been whispering and laughing, but when they saw her, they shut up. *Were they laughing at me?* she wondered, the tears stinging again.

I'm messing up here, I'm messing up at home, I'm messing up everything! Dana locked herself into a stall and burst into tears.

Chapter
Three

Jessica stood in the doorway of Tristan's office, hoping he'd look up and see her. She wasn't sure if she should knock on the half-open door or just announce herself. Tristan seemed angry about something; he sat at his desk slamming papers around, muttering.

"Excuse me," she said, and he glanced up at her. "I'm Jessica Wakefield. I don't know if you remember me, but I'm in your art-history discussion class."

"Of course I remember you, Jessica," he said with a warm smile, pushing aside the papers as he stood. He extended his hand, which she shook. *Nice firm handshake,* she noticed. Tingles actually skittered up her arm. "Second row, right?" he added, and Jessica nodded, trying to keep her expression from showing how much that pleased her. *He did notice me!* she thought. "Have a seat," he told her, gesturing at the leather chair facing his desk.

"You said we could stop by anytime if we had questions or a problem," Jessica began, but she noticed Tristan's attention had been diverted by someone standing in the doorway. She turned around. It was Dr. Devane.

"Tristan, have you finished critiquing that article?" the intimidating professor asked. "And I also need the scheduling information about our visiting lecturer from Tulane."

"I've got both right here." While Tristan opened his knapsack and took out a folder, Dr. Devane gave Jessica a curt nod.

"Dr. Devane, your lecture yesterday was so interesting," she said.

His response was a tight smile.

"I bet students say stuff like that all the time to get on your good side, huh?" she rushed to add, his lack of conversation making her feel stupid.

"No, actually they don't," he replied. "And you are?"

"Jessica Wakefield. I'm an art-history major."

"Well, Miss Wakefield, what can we do for you this afternoon?"

"I came to talk to Tristan—I mean, Mr. Patterson."

Tristan handed a large envelope to Dr. Devane. "Miss Wakefield arrived just a moment before you,

50

Dr. Devane. We didn't have the opportunity to discuss the reason for her visit."

They both stared at her, and Jessica gulped. She hadn't planned on approaching Tristan with an audience. "Well, see, I've, um—I have a lot of questions from the lecture and from today's discussion section."

Dr. Devane nodded. He put the envelope Tristan had given him into his briefcase, then he left.

Tristan picked up a yellow pad from his desk and scribbled something on it, then tore off the sheet and handed it to Jessica. "Here's a short list of some terrific books on art history—not stuffy textbooks," he added with a smile. "You can find them at the library."

Hmmm . . . Does this mean he's not interested? she wondered. She glanced at the list, then looked up at Tristan. "Um, I appreciate this, but, well, I was thinking I might need more hands-on help, like tutoring, maybe?"

"Tutoring on top of discussion section and the lectures?" he said. "That's quite a lot of art history for one student with other classes."

He's not interested, she thought, her heart sinking. *First he directs me to the library, and now he's pointing out how tutoring might be overkill.*

"But if you're that committed, I'd be happy to tutor you," he continued. "It'll have to be during my office hours, though. Does that work with your schedule?"

"Um, yes," she replied. *I'll make it work!*

"Why don't we say Monday at . . . " She loved the way he bit his bottom lip as he concentrated on his calendar. "Let's say . . . ten o'clock?"

How are you supposed to dress to be tutored? she wondered.

Nina knew that jabbing the arrow-shaped button over and over wouldn't make the elevator come any faster, but it made her feel better. According to students coming out of the stairwell, some inconsiderate girl was holding up the elevator on the fourth floor. Probably some sorority sister waiting for fifteen friends. Nina looked at the stairwell door and groaned. She was way too tired to even consider dragging her tired body up six flights. After back-to-back classes all day long, she had only two hours to rest up before she had to be at work at the lab.

I have only myself to blame, she reminded herself. *I was the one who decided that keeping myself swamped with classes and work was the best way to get over Bryan.* She frowned just thinking of his name. . . . *That lying, sneaking, two-timing* . . . Her thoughts were interrupted as the elevator finally opened and a pack of chattering girls stampeded off, practically knocking her down.

"Well, excuuuuse me," Nina grumbled. She slipped into the elevator and hit six. *Finally.*

But the elevator hardly moved before it stopped again. She looked at the panel. Second floor! *Memo to the resident board: There should be a law that people who live on the second floor are required to use the stairs at all times.*

The door slid open, and a girl stood there, gawking at Nina.

Definitely a freshman, Nina said to herself.

"Going down?" the girl asked with a bright smile.

"No, up," Nina explained.

"Oh." The girl got on anyway. "I'm on my way to the bookstore—do you think they're still open?"

Nina looked at her watch. "I think they closed at five," she said.

"Oh," the girl replied. The elevator stopped at Nina's floor. "Oh, cool, this is the floor with the suites and singles!" The freshman peeked out into the hallway. "It must be so great to have a room to yourself."

"Yeah," Nina said. *If I didn't have the suitemate from hell.* "Well, see you later," she added as the door whooshed closed.

Her stomach growled as she fished her key out of her knapsack. Nina had a box of cereal and a pint of skim milk in the fridge—the perfect snack before a little nap. Her mood instantly perked up at the thought of both. She said a silent prayer that Shondra would be out—her suite-mate had gone from a sweet but annoying boyfriend-obsessed girl to a total lunatic when that boyfriend had broken up with her a few days ago.

She pushed open the door to the small common room between her bedroom and Shondra's and stopped dead in her tracks. Everything was covered in plastic wrap. The futon, the lamp, the television and VCR, the bookshelf . . . *everything!* Even her potted philodendron. And in the middle of the floor Shondra was kneeling over a ring of black and red candles—chanting, Nina realized.

"Oh my God," Nina said slowly, staring at Shondra.

"Shhh—" Shondra whirled around and glared at her. "The spell book says absolute silence is required." Closing her eyes, Shondra turned back to the candle ring, held out her arms, and moaned.

Of all the people at SVU, I get stuck with a psycho, Nina lamented. She flicked on the lights, which wasn't easy since the switch-plate cover was also plastic wrapped. "Shondra, I don't even want to know what you're doing, but try not to set the place on fire, okay?" Stepping around her crazy suite-mate, she bent over the futon and saw her lab coat and notebook buried under the plastic wrap. She started peeling a corner of it away.

"Noooooooo!" Shondra leaped to her feet and

grabbed Nina's wrist with both hands. "Don't disturb the protective sheath."

Nina shook herself loose. "Shondra, I'm not in the mood, and I don't have time for this."

"You're the one who told me I had to deal with getting dumped, *Nina*," Shondra spat. "The book I got says you have to purify bad karma before it escapes and does major damage."

Nina reached beneath the plastic wrap and snatched her lab coat and notebook. "Listen, Shondra. Your ex-boyfriend *and* his karma have already escaped." *Luckily for him,* she added mentally.

"Yeah, thanks to you." Shondra yanked the plastic from the futon and wadded it into a ball. "You just destroyed the whole aura in the room. Now I have to start all over. You're really supportive, Nina."

Nina walked into her room and slammed the door shut. She leaned back against it, letting out the breath she'd been holding. *What am I going to do? One of these days I'm going to come home and find that kook stabbing pins into voodoo dolls and beheading live chickens.*

Nina dropped onto her bed and hugged her pillow against her. So much for that cereal or a nap. She pulled out her to-do list. In capital letters across the top she added: HOUSING OFFICE—ROOM SWITCH.

*   *   *

Expecting to find Sam and his slacker friends hogging the living room when she got home, Elizabeth was surprised to see Jessica sitting on the sofa and the room quiet. Jessica had a notebook in her lap and a huge textbook open on the coffee table in front of her.

"What are you doing?" Elizabeth asked, staring at her sister.

"What does it look like?" Jessica replied, glancing up. "I'm studying. And I'll have you know, I've read six pages beyond my actual assignment."

Elizabeth stepped over Sam's in-line skates, knelt in front of Jessica, and put her hand on her sister's forehead. "You don't feel overly warm, so you can't be delirious from a fever."

"I can vouch for her," Neil said, coming through the swinging kitchen door. The smell of spaghetti wafted in behind him. "She's been sitting on that couch for over an hour with her nose in that book."

"Jessica Wakefield, my twin sister." Elizabeth sat down next to Jessica. "Studying? Reading beyond her assignment? Spending her evening with a textbook?"

"Elizabeth, give Jess some credit," Neil said, sitting down on the window seat.

"Yeah, and give Jess some *quiet* too," Jessica told them, picking up her textbook and shifting it to her lap. "I know you're going to find this hard to believe, Liz, but I actually *like* this stuff.

It's interesting. Did you know that aesthetics is the study of the nature of beauty and art?"

"Wow," Elizabeth said, truly impressed. "You really do sound into it. And throwing around words like *aesthetics*, no less. I have to say, I'm proud of you."

Jessica wrapped Elizabeth into a hug. "Thanks, Liz. Now, if you guys don't mind?" Jessica turned her attention back to her notebook.

Elizabeth stared at her twin. Then it came to her. Jessica might be able to fool Neil, who despite being Jessica's best friend would never know her like Elizabeth did. Maybe Jessica really was into art history. Maybe. But Elizabeth would bet her last buck that Jessica's new study habits had something to do with a guy.

Chapter Four

"I can't tell you his name—*yet*." Jessica broke off a piece of her blueberry-and-banana muffin and popped it in her mouth, then sat back on the plush sofa in the Theta house living room.

"Why not?" Lila Fowler asked, pouring herself a cup of coffee. "He's not some nerd you're too embarrassed to admit you like, is he?"

Hardly, Jessica thought with a smile as Tristan's anything-but-nerdlike face and physique came into her mind. She really shouldn't be talking about him, she knew, but Jessica couldn't help it. Today was only Wednesday, and there were so many days to get through before Monday for their tutoring session. How could she not at least mention to her best friends that she'd *met* the greatest guy?

She'd almost slipped to Elizabeth last night after they finished studying. When Elizabeth had gotten over her shock at seeing Jessica with a textbook, Elizabeth had brought down her books and the two of them had studied together in total silence for about two hours. Until the past couple of days Jessica had never understood how her sister could stand that—sitting in a quiet room and reading a textbook, taking notes, getting up only to brew a pot of coffee or stretch. But now Jessica herself was doing just that. It was unbelievable how she was changing. Changing so much that she knew she should keep her hopes for her TA to herself.

"So do we know him?" Denise Waters asked.

"I don't think so," Jessica replied. None of her friends took art history. "And *no*, Lila, he's not a nerd—try the furthest thing from it." She grinned. "I'm afraid I'll jinx it if I talk too much about him. He hasn't *officially* asked me out on a real date."

"Sophomore?" Alexandra Rollins asked.

"*Grad* student," Jessica replied.

"Ah," Lila said, smiling. "An older man. Good going."

"So where'd you meet him? Starlights?" Denise asked. Starlights was their favorite new nightclub on campus.

"Nope," Jessica told her. "I . . . met him in the arts building." Well, that was true. She could just imagine the snickers and giggles she'd get if she mentioned she'd met him in class and that he was her TA. They'd make all sorts of immature assumptions about trying to score an A.

"Well, I want the dirt the minute he asks you out," Lila demanded. "And if you need advice about handling older men, you know who to come to."

"There is definitely something about an older guy," Alexandra said. "A freshman in my bio class keeps staring at me—I think he has a crush on me. But dating a freshman seems so weird when you're a sophomore."

"Not to change the subject, but speaking of *freshmen*," Denise said, "we really have to start planning for rush week. And Jessica, it's official now— you're on the ballot for pledge chairwoman."

On the ballot. For an elected position in Theta. It was unreal. Last week Jessica had been shocked when Lila, Alexandra, and Denise, who were sure to be voted in as the new government, had suggested she run for pledge chairwoman. She was still unable to believe her name had been tossed around for a position of responsibility. And now she was officially on the ballot.

"Denise," Jessica said, "if in a millionth chance I actually *did* win, do you really think I'd do a good job? I mean, it'd be really bad if I let *you* down—we're friends, you know?" Denise was officially acting president until the elections were held in two weeks, and then she'd be president. No one was running against Denise for the top job—

61

everyone liked and respected her that much.

"I think you'd do a great job, Jess," Denise replied. "So when this amazing new guy of yours does ask you out, just don't forget us, okay? We need you!"

We need you. Jessica felt a rush of emotion hit in her chest and a little sting in the backs of her eyes. That was the first time anyone had ever said that to her.

Elizabeth fanned herself with her notebook. Although her attic room was cozy and airy, it had one major drawback. At certain times of the day—like right now—the sun streamed through the big dormer window at just the right angle to give her a sunburn. Plus the late afternoon sun's glare was so strong that she couldn't even see her journalism textbook. There was no way she'd get any studying done up here.

But that was what was so great about living in her own house—she didn't have to sit here blinded by the sun or in a little dorm room or go to the library. She had a whole house at her disposal. The window seat in the living room would be the perfect place to curl up with her book and a giant glass of iced tea. She gathered her stuff and headed down the narrow stairs.

The moment she reached the second-floor

hallway between Jessica's and Neil's rooms, she knew her plan to study in the living room was doomed.

Sam and his friend, who for some reason was named Bugsy, were hunched over a video game about six inches from the television. They were both so into it that neither of them even acknowledged her as she came down the stairs.

She headed into the kitchen and plunked her books on the table. A small gob of grape jelly flew at her, landing on her new SVU sweatshirt. Furious, Elizabeth picked up her books and turned them over. The back of her sixty-dollar journalism textbook was smeared with jelly.

I am going to kill him! Turning to the sink for a rag, she stared in shock at the mountain of dirty dishes stacked there. How could so many dishes have piled up since she and Neil cleaned up the kitchen last night? Elizabeth never left her own dirty dishes in the sink—she always washed them right after she finished eating. But some people in this house were inconsiderate slobs. "Like *you*, Sam!" she shouted over her shoulder. She yanked open the cabinet under the sink and grabbed a sponge and cleanser. She furiously cleaned off the table and her book, then dabbed at her sweatshirt with a wet paper towel.

Sitting on one of the stools, she opened the book, uncapped her pink highlighter, and bowed her head over the second chapter of the *Complete History of American Journalism*.

"Whoo-hoo!" Bugsy's victory cry made him sound like a demented owl. *Ignore it,* she told herself. *Concentrate.* "Whoo-hoo *squared,* buddy! You're about to lose, man!"

Elizabeth laid her head against her book. There was no way she could study with that idiot shrieking.

"Foul! Foul!" Bugsy's voice boomed. "No one beats the Bug Man at Holographic B-Ball. I'm the Orange County champ!"

"Prepare for extermination, Bug Man!" Sam shouted. "He shoots. He sinks it. He scores!"

Elizabeth stomped to the door and pushed it open. "Hey, Sam!"

No response. They were either making too much noise to hear her or totally ignoring her. She leaned her head through the doorway and cupped her hand around her mouth. "Sam! Could you keep it down? I'm trying to study in here."

Without taking his eyes from the screen, Sam waved over one shoulder.

Well, at least he deigned to acknowledge my existence. She let the door swing shut.

"Ha! Got you again!" Sam screeched before Elizabeth even made it back to the table. Then he began a rousing verse of some vulgar victory song. Bugsy joined in, painfully off-key.

The muscles of her jaws were clenched so tightly, it was giving her a headache. Sam was just too much! Everywhere she turned, something about him infuriated her. From his dirty dishes in the sink to his junky boxes that littered the whole downstairs, Sam was a nightmare as a housemate. She used to think Jessica was bad when they shared a dorm room, but compared to Sam, Jessica was a neat freak.

Elizabeth pushed open the kitchen door and poked her head through. "Sam! Give me a break!"

"Bugsy, man, you have got to see this girl in my communications class—she is the hottest thing I've ever seen. She's like a 36D and—"

Okay, that's it. I've had it!

She shoved through the swinging door. "Sam!" Again no response. "Sam, I'm warning you," she growled, marching over to where he was sprawled. "Ow!" she screamed as her foot hit a cardboard box of Sam's unpacked junk. She lost her balance and flung out her hands to steady herself, only to land them on top of an open box containing the rest of his precious beer-can collection. There was a crashing, crunching noise and pain shot through her hand.

"Oowww!" she cried, struggling to her knees. When she lifted her hand from the box, a scarlet stream trickled from her palm down her wrist, running all the way to her elbow.

Sam got to his feet and ran over to her. "Liz? Are you okay?"

"Man, she's bleeding everywhere!" Bugsy said.

"Oh, so now you're paying attention to me?" Elizabeth yelled at him. "Just stay away from me!" Sam took a step back, and Elizabeth saw the flash of concern in his hazel eyes.

"What the hell is going on up here?" Neil asked, coming up the stairs from the basement, where the washer and dryer were. "Oh my God, Elizabeth!" He dropped his laundry basket and was suddenly at her side, pressing a white T-shirt to her hand.

"Neil, your clean shirt! It'll be ruined," Elizabeth protested.

"Don't worry about it." Neil led her over to the stairs and lowered her to a sitting position on the bottom step. "I'm going to gently remove the shirt and take a look at your hand, okay?" He sounded like a surgeon removing bandages.

"Neil, I'm sure it's no big deal—just a cut," she said, though it hurt like hell. She glared at Sam, who had the decency to still look ashamed.

"This looks pretty deep to me," Neil said. "It may need stitches."

"Stitches?" Elizabeth croaked. "No way."

"No way you're *not* going to the ER, Liz," Neil insisted, guiding her up by the elbow. "Canedge cuts can be serious." He folded the once-white T-shirt and pressed it against her hand again. "Here, hold this." He brushed his hair out of his gray eyes and then checked his pocket for his car keys. "Can you walk to the car?"

"Of course I can walk," Elizabeth said. But her legs were more wobbly than she thought. She caught Neil's arm.

"Are you parked behind me?" Neil asked Bugsy.

"I was just leaving, man." The very pale Bugsy slipped out the door ahead of them and dashed to his car.

"I can take her," Sam told Neil. "It was my fault."

"That's the first honest thing you've said since you moved in," Elizabeth snarled. "But I'd rather Neil took me. You've already done more than enough."

Please be at a class, Chloe prayed as she headed down the hall toward her dorm room. She wasn't in the mood to deal with Moira. Although her roommate did seem to have something resembling a grudging respect for her now that Chloe supposedly had Tom Watts for a boyfriend, Moira was still ice-cold. The girl lived to embarrass Chloe, especially in front of others.

Chloe's heart sank when she saw that the door to her room was half open. She heard laughter and figured Moira was hanging out with her friends. Well, at least Chloe wouldn't be trapped alone with Moira. For such a bitch, Moira had nice friends, and they seemed to really like Chloe. And that was all Chloe wanted. To be liked, to be accepted, to make friends. Right now, lying was the only way Chloe could make friends. But once people got to know her and like her, she wouldn't have to spin story after story.

As she got closer, she heard a low, sexy male voice coming from her room—a voice that sounded like Tom's. Was Tom in there? she wondered. That would be so perfect! He'd come to see her just when Moira and all her friends were there!

She paused outside the door and trained her ear toward his voice.

". . . I'll see you. . . ."

It *was* Tom's voice! *Yes!* Chloe was about to head in when she realized his voice had been drowned out by laughter—a lot of laughter. Tom wasn't so funny. What were they all laughing at?

"Play it again!" a girl's voice shrieked with delight.

"And turn it up, Moira," another girl added. "I can barely hear it."

Huh? What was going on? Chloe inched closer to the edge of the door and flattened herself against the wall. She heard the answering machine whir as it rewound and then click to play. Tom's voice floated into the hallway. "*Uh . . . listen, Cody. This is Tom. . . .*"

Chloe winced. Tom's voice was nothing more than a message on the answering machine. And he'd actually called her by the wrong name! She put her hand on the wall to support her wobbly knees and leaned closer.

Jill shrieked, "Wait, wait! Start it over. I want to hear that part again."

The machine went through its motions. "*Uh . . . listen, Cody. This is Tom. . . .*" It sounded even worse the second time.

"Do you think he got hit on the head with a football, and that's why our brilliant quarterback can't remember his girlfriend's name?" Moira's voice was full of victory.

Chloe heard a bunch of different girls' laughter, then quiet as Tom's voice continued in the same impersonal tone. "*. . . I got your message . . . um, messages . . . and look, uh, thanks for the invites . . . and I did have a good time last week too, but, um . . . I'm sort of seeing someone now and . . . it was nice to see you again after so long, so, uh, take care, Cody. Bye.*" Click.

"*Cody!*" Moira announced in triumph. "Is that the best or what? Can someone please tell me how I got stuck with the world's biggest loser as a roommate?"

"Well, she's definitely the world's biggest *liar*." Eva Bedford sounded sort of sad.

Chloe closed her eyes. Her face was burning,

her heart was racing, and her stomach was churning so fast, she thought she'd be sick.

They got her. There was no way out of this, no lies to spin. The minute they got tired of replaying the message, they'd tell everyone in Oakley about it, invite everyone to listen to it.

Chloe turned and ran for the stairs before anyone could see her.

Chapter Five

The automatic glass doors of the emergency-room entrance whooshed open, and Elizabeth stepped forward. But when the cold, antiseptic-smelling air hit her, her knees turned to rubber bands. Suddenly the edges of her field of vision started to narrow, as if someone were drawing a black curtain in from both sides of her face. She slid to the tile floor in slow motion.

"Elizabeth!" Neil grabbed her under the arms and lifted.

"I'm okay," she muttered, grabbing at his strong arms for support. "I . . . just need . . . to . . . sit down for a second."

"You *are* sitting—right in the doorway." He hauled her the rest of the way to her feet. "Come on. Let's get you to a chair."

As he settled her into one of the plastic orange

chairs, she saw a reddish smear on the sleeve of his shirt. "Now I've ruined two of your shirts," she said.

Neil smiled. "Don't worry about my stupid shirts. I'm gonna go sign you in." He walked over to the desk and came back a few minutes later with a clipboard that had a pen dangling from a cord. "Okay, we have to fill this out," he told her, sitting back down next to her. "Name . . . address . . . " He wrote quickly but neatly on the form. "Social security number?" Elizabeth told him, and he scribbled it down. "Nature of wound, deep cut to left hand . . . Insurance?" Elizabeth managed to reach into her purse and pull out her insurance card. "Okay, I'll take this stuff back over to the desk."

Neil returned and sat down next to her. "I hope they don't make you wait too long," he said. "I'm really worried about that cut."

Elizabeth leaned her head against Neil's shoulder. "Thanks for all your help, Neil," she told him. "I really appreciate it. You're not missing a class because of me, are you?"

"Oh, just my favorite one, physics!" Neil said with a grin. "I should be thanking *you* for the excuse to blow it off."

"This is all Sam's fault!" Elizabeth exploded. "Thanks to him, you're missing class and I'm bleeding to death! If he'd unpacked his stupid boxes and put his junk away—" She glanced at the big round clock on the wall—"I would have been done with my journalism assignment and halfway through poli sci by now."

"Yeah, and I'd be suffering through physics," Neil said. "Keep your arm elevated, Liz," he added. "And forget Sam. Don't even think about him."

"I don't know how much longer I can take him," she complained, resting her head against the wall. "He's a total slob, he's obnoxious, and he's inconsiderate of everyone else's property, space, and feelings. Now you know why I was worried about him moving in."

Neil leaned his head back too and sighed. "I know Sam's not the easiest person to cohabit with, but he's a good guy underneath that slacker-jerk exterior—you know that. Liz, you're always gonna have problems living with someone if you expect them to meet your standards of what's right and wrong."

She sat up straight and turned to face him. "*My* standards of right and wrong? Neil, what's *right* about leaving dishes piled up in the sink? Boxes all over the place? Hogging the living room, blasting the stereo, eating other people's food, being obnoxious every single second? How are those *my* standards?"

"I'm not saying *he's* right or that *it's* right,"

Neil responded. "Liz!" he snapped, "you're not *elevating!*" She lifted her arm. "I'm just saying you have to learn to get along with him, that's all."

"Well, unless they offer How to Live with an Obnoxious Jerk as a class at SVU, I guess I'll just have to muddle through," Elizabeth said, her hand suddenly throbbing worse. It was hard to keep it lifted up so high.

"That's my girl," Neil replied. "*Elevate*, Liz!" he yelled as she rested her injured hand on her thigh. "Elevate!"

"Wakefield, Elizabeth?" a nurse called out.

"Finally!" she muttered. Neil helped her up and led her over to the nurse.

"Ooh, that's some cut," the woman said after she removed Neil's makeshift bandage. "Don't worry, hon. We'll get you stitched up good."

Stitched up good? Sam was toast.

Chloe wiped her tear-streaked face with the sleeve of her T-shirt and sniffed.

The shrub-lined alleyway beside the library was the perfect place to wallow in misery in total privacy. She'd blown it, big time. How was she supposed to walk into Oakley ever again? How could she ever face Eva, Lisa, Anoushka, and all the other girls? And how could she deal with Moira reveling in Chloe's humiliation?

She wished she had a tissue so she could blow her nose and dry her eyes, but she didn't know if she could risk dashing into the library to get to the bathroom. What if she ran into someone from her dorm? She was sure that in the half hour that had passed since she'd run off, Moira had played that message for everyone in Oakley.

Chloe peeked through the bushes to see if anyone from her dorm was around.

The only person Chloe recognized on the path to the library was Jessica Wakefield. Just the sight of perfect Jessica made Chloe tear up again. The blonde looked totally happy. Chloe could tell that Jessica was the kind of girl who had a million friends and two million guys chasing after her. And on top of it, Jessica was actually nice. *If I could befriend Jessica, all my problems would be solved.*

Wait a minute! Chloe thought. *We're already sort of friends! If I have those art-history notes I borrowed, I can grab her now, ask her to wait till I make a copy, and then invite her for a coffee or something as a thank-you.*

Chloe tore open her knapsack and pulled out her art-history notebook, then dusted herself off and climbed out from behind the bushes. Jessica was just a few feet ahead of her now on the path.

"Jessica? Jessica, right?" Chloe called, and

Jessica turned around, staring at Chloe as if trying to place her.

"It's me, Chloe, from art history? I borrowed your notes yesterday, remember? I was just going inside to make a copy. I'm so sorry I didn't get them back to you today in the lecture hall—I actually forgot I had them!"

"Oh, no problem," Jessica told her with a smile. "But I could use them before tomorrow's discussion session, so I'll just come with you to the copier." Chloe smiled too and held open the library door. "I think the copier is on the second floor," Jessica said. "My feet are killing me from these stupid new sandals—do you mind if we wait for the elevator?"

"Not at all—I know exactly what you mean," Chloe said, thrilled at how great this was going. She and Jessica were chatting like friends! "I live on the third floor of my dorm, and so I usually just run up and down the stairs, like ten times a day. My feet are always killing me." Actually Chloe always took the elevator, but it seemed a good way to bring up Oakley—to make sure Jessica didn't live there too. If Jessica did and heard about the Tom thing, she'd never be seen talking to Chloe again.

"I'm so glad I'm out of the dorms," Jessica said, pushing the elevator's up button. "I lived in Dickenson with my sister last year, but now we have our own place off campus. Total freedom!"

"You're so lucky!" Chloe exclaimed, relieved. "I live in Oakley. Do you still hang out with anyone from the dorms?" *Please say no.*

"Actually no," Jessica replied. "My friends all live in Theta house. That's my sorority and—" Jessica broke off to wave at two trendy-looking girls who were coming down the stairs.

"I have a friend in Theta," Chloe said very casually. "Lila Fowler?"

"Ohmigod!" Jessica shouted, and got a dirty look from the librarian at the main desk. Jessica turned to Chloe with a huge smile. *"Oops,"* she whispered. "Lila is my *best friend* from home! Where do you know her from?"

"Her family and mine are old friends," Chloe replied, relieved that she was actually telling the truth. "I don't know Lila too well, though."

The elevator opened, and a crowd emerged. Chloe and Jessica stepped in. "Well, I hope you're considering rushing Theta," Jessica said. "It's the best sorority on campus, and now you already know two sisters—Lila and me!"

Theta. It figured that the very sorority she was practically being *asked* to pledge was her *mother's* sorority. Her mom *expected* her to join, which was the major reason Chloe didn't want to. She'd vowed to live by her own rules when she arrived at

SVU. Be her own person instead of the spoiled rich girl her mother wanted her to enjoy being.

But trading designer clothes for her worn corduroys and ratty T-shirts hadn't fooled Moira—she'd pegged Chloe as a rich girl disguised in "I'm-so-down-to-earth" rags in two seconds flat. But Chloe *wasn't* in disguise. The way she dressed totally reflected her personality, the way she felt. This was who she wanted to be.

Still, if friendship lay in pledging Theta, then that's what Chloe would do.

"My mom was a Theta," Chloe told Jessica, following her out of the elevator. "She'd be thrilled if I joined."

Jessica stopped and grabbed Chloe's wrist. "That means you're a legacy!" Jessica exclaimed. "So if you pledge, you're pretty much in unless all the sisters hate your guts or you mess up the pledge requirements or something. Hey, did they move the copier?" Jessica asked, looking around. "Oh, there it is." They walked toward the machine, which had a small line of people waiting to use it.

"So joining a sorority must be a really great way to make friends," Chloe said as they waited. "Especially for a freshman."

"Definitely," Jessica replied.

"Look, guys, there's Cody!"

Oh, no. That was definitely Moira's voice.

Don't look up, Chloe told herself. *Just pretend you don't hear her.*

"*Oh, Co-dy!*" Moira singsonged.

"This is a library, miss!" hissed a clerk.

Chloe dared a look toward where the voices had come from. The girls had gone. "Jessica, can I be really honest?" Chloe asked. "I don't want to sound like some pathetic eager freshman, but . . . joining Theta is like my *dream* in life. You have no idea how much becoming a Theta means to me."

Jessica was beaming. Chloe had said the right thing—for once.

"And not to sound even more pathetic," Chloe added as she reached the head of the copier line, "but I can't even believe you're so nice—you're like this sophisticated sophomore in the best sorority on campus, and here you are, being really nice to me, just some freshman you don't even really know, letting me copy your notes, spending so much time talking to me about Theta. . . . "

"Hey," Jessica said with a bright smile, "I just thought of something. I'm planning on going to Theta house—I just need to stop home first. How about you come with me? I can introduce you around."

Chloe suddenly realized that saying the *right* thing was much more valuable than lying. Nothing Chloe had said was a lie—she'd just exaggerated a little. And suddenly her new best friend to be was Jessica Wakefield!

The minute Moira and everyone on her floor saw her hanging out with Jessica, they'd stop the Cody stuff real fast.

Why do they always keep these little rooms so cold? Elizabeth wondered. She shivered and shifted on the paper-covered table in the small examination room. The paper stuck to her jeans and crinkled noisily. It had been at least ten minutes since Nurse Williams had taken her blood pressure and temperature. Where was the doctor already?

As if on cue, there was a knock at the door and then a man in a white lab coat came in. "Hi, there," he said. "I'm Dr. Ahmed. Did you think we'd forgotten you?" He washed his hands and slipped on latex gloves. "Now, let's have a look at that hand. Oh"—he checked his clipboard— "Elizabeth, I hope you don't mind my friend here observing. Finn Robinson is a medical student following me on my rounds today."

"No, not at all," Elizabeth murmured, unable to take her eyes off Finn Robinson. Tall and blond, Finn was one of the best-looking guys Elizabeth had ever seen. He looked like a cross between a brilliant intellectual and a California surfer. She barely felt the doctor poking at her cut.

Was Finn a med student at SVU? she wondered

"Nasty little cut," the doctor said. "From?"

"Beer can," Elizabeth said without thinking, instantly regretting it when Finn smiled. *Now he thinks I'm some partying undergrad who chugs beer in the middle of the day and gets drunk enough to cut myself!* She rushed to change his impression. "One of my housemates has this collection of international beer cans, you know, from around the world, places he's visited," Elizabeth rambled. *Just shut up!*

"When was your last tetanus shot?" The doctor drizzled some sort of smelly antiseptic across her palm.

If Elizabeth had to have another tetanus shot, Sam was really dead meat! "Not long ago. Last spring."

"Good enough," he said, and Elizabeth breathed a sigh of relief. Finn smiled again. Another private little smile. Blushing, she darted her gaze back to her hand. "Just a few stitches, and you'll heal fine," Dr. Ahmed announced. "Finn, you can help me out by holding her hand firmly."

Elizabeth stiffened. He was going to touch her . . . hold her hand. *Firmly.* As he stepped closer to her, Elizabeth closed her eyes, overwhelmed by a strange rush of sensations racing through her. Her eyes popped open as a strong, warm hand closed around her wrist. She glanced up at Finn, and he smiled at her, a sweet smile, an everything's-going-to-be-okay smile. A guy hadn't affected her like this in forever. Since . . . since this past summer and Sam, if she had to admit it. But Sam had made it clear he was a jerk right away, whereas Finn seemed very mature, very sophisticated. Very unjerklike.

His eyes weren't brown as she'd thought—they were a dark gold, like antique brass. Suddenly she wished she were wearing something more attractive than a jelly-stained SVU sweat-shirt and jeans.

As Finn's grip on her wrist tightened, a tingle ran up her arm to the back of her neck. She barely felt the shot the doctor gave her to deaden her pain. She barely felt anything at all . . . just the pressure of Finn's fingers against her skin.

"All done." Doctor Ahmed snipped the last piece of suture thread. "The nurse will come back with instructions for the next few days," he told her, "and then you're free to go."

Finn gently rested her hand against her thigh, and when he moved away from her to follow the doctor out, her hand felt cold. Suddenly it throbbed. He turned in the doorway to smile at her. "Take care of yourself."

Smile, she ordered herself. *Flirt. Let him know you're interested! Do something, you idiot!*

Elizabeth smiled, that tight smile that plastered

on her lips whenever she felt awkward. And then Finn was gone. *Great,* she thought. *He already thinks you're just a typical undergrad who cuts your hand on beer cans and wears stained sweatshirts. And now he knows you're too unsophisticated to even smile naturally.*

Why can't you be more like Jessica? Elizabeth yelled at herself, looking down at the tiny stitches and wriggling her hand. Her sister would have smiled, flirted, and giggled during the entire procedure—Jessica would have left here with a date or at least an "I'll call you." All Elizabeth was leaving with was a stiff hand.

Be more like Jessica. Interesting, Elizabeth thought. Until just recently, the thought of being anything like Jessica was scary. Not take school seriously? Be obsessed with fashion and makeup trends? Be guy crazy and totally impulsive? But lately Elizabeth had been envying Jessica her ability to go after what she wanted. Jessica had *guts.* Her twin wouldn't be afraid to flirt for fear of making a fool of herself if the guy wasn't interested. Jessica would just chalk it up to him being gay or married, whereas Elizabeth would feel rejected. *Jessica has confidence,* Elizabeth realized. *Confidence.*

And Jessica seems to be changing—or at least trying to, Elizabeth thought. *Maybe it's time I tried to change a little too. Not be so serious all the time. Flirt when the guy of my dreams is actually standing next to me, holding my hand.* Now she'd never see Finn again. Not that she'd ever get his face out of her mind.

The nurse returned with Elizabeth's instructions on caring for her hand, then left her alone. Elizabeth hopped off the examination table. Her hand felt like lead.

"Elizabeth?"

She looked up, and there he was, standing in the doorway. Her breath actually stopped for a second. *Don't blow this,* she warned herself.

"Dr. Ahmed asked me to make sure you have someone to drive you home," he said. "You're more disoriented than you may realize right now."

"Oh, um, yes—my housemate's waiting for me," she replied. *"Oh, um"* . . . *Is that how you learned to communicate in your public-speaking course last year?*

"Great. Well, take care," he told her.

Elizabeth, say something, say something, say something. Anything.

"Do you go to SVU?" she asked just as he turned to walk away.

He turned back and stood in the doorway. "Yes," he said, his perfect smile revealing a dimple in his left cheek. "I'm first year. Dr. Ahmed is a friend of mine, so he's letting me observe some of his minor cases in the ER today and tomorrow."

"I'm at SVU too," she told him. "I guess my SVU sweatshirt gives that away, huh?" She laughed, feeling like the biggest idiot in the world. *I have to start watching Jessica in action,* she thought. *I have to learn how to flirt.*

"So, I was thinking . . . ," he said, and Elizabeth's hope skyrocketed. *Please be thinking of asking for my telephone number.* "I'd love to follow up on how your hand's healing, so, if you'd like to give me your telephone number . . . "

Yes! How she actually managed to interest Finn with her stupid comments, awkward smile, and kiddie outfit was beyond her. He must be a really genuine guy, she realized. Not pretentious or stuck-up.

Suddenly Elizabeth relaxed. Finn might be a sophisticated, older med student, but he clearly liked her. Sensed that she was serious and mature, that they probably had a lot in common, even though she was just an undergrad. She smiled at him—a Jessica smile that came naturally this time.

She scribbled her first name and number on the back of a gauze wrapper and handed it to him.

Finn folded it and tucked it into his back pocket, then smiled and left. Elizabeth hadn't felt this happy in—she didn't even know how long.

"That nurse told me I could come help you out," Neil said, poking his head into the room. He looked at her for a second. "Hey, what did they give you?"

"Ten stitches," she said as he took her arm and guided her out.

"No, I mean what drugs?" he asked. "With that sappy, happy look on your face, I figure they pumped you full of some miracle painkiller."

"The best kind too," Elizabeth told him. *Tall, blond, gorgeous, and smart.*

Sam lay on the huge daisy-print sofa in the living room, flicking through the channels with the remote control. Nothing on. He checked his watch again. *How long does it take to get a bandage stuck on your hand?* he wondered. Neil and Elizabeth had been gone for almost two hours. *Maybe she did really hurt herself,* he thought, feeling like a jerk.

Well, maybe if she wasn't so into telling him and everyone else what they could and couldn't do, she wouldn't have gotten herself hurt in the first place. *Sam, turn the music down. . . . Sam, can't you shut up? . . . Sam, you're not gonna leave that there, are you? Sam, Sam, Sam . . .* It went on and on. His own mother hadn't been that bad. Then again, Sam's mother hadn't exactly ever washed a dish in her very wealthy life. And the succession of nannies who'd raised Sam weren't allowed to tell him what to do or how to do it. The only person other than

Elizabeth who liked telling Sam what to do was his dad, which was the main reason he didn't spend too much time visiting the family mansion.

He heard a car door slam and two sets of footsteps coming up the path. Sam felt the wall coming down around him, the wall that kept Elizabeth Wakefield from ever getting too close. He did give a damn, actually, that she'd hurt herself because of him. That her hand was bleeding, that she might have needed stitches. That she was *hurt,* period. He did care. But hell if he'd let her see that. She'd take it and use it against him somehow, some way.

He thought about opening the door for them but stayed where he was, remote control in hand. He glued his eyes to the screen, some nature show about dinosaurs.

"That's Sam on the sofa," he heard Jessica say. "Isn't that couch fabulous? It's so retro. And we got it for like nothing at the Salvation Army."

Sam relaxed. It was only Jessica and some friend of hers. *What is taking Elizabeth so long?* he wondered.

Sam turned to nod at the friend, who was really cute. Not Jessica's usual fashion-victim type, he noted. This girl was natural and seemed cool. Straight red-brown hair, hardly any makeup, and a white V-necked T-shirt, baggy jeans, and funky red sneakers.

"Hi, Sam," the girl said.

"Sam, this is my friend Chloe Murphy," Jessica

said. "She's only a freshman, so don't scare her away while I go upstairs to change. Be nice, polite, and friendly." Jessica ran up the stairs.

"Boo!" he whispered at Chloe. She giggled and sat down on the sofa next to his feet. "Oh, no, did I scare you? Are you gonna run back home to mama?" he teased.

"Now, *that* would be scary," Chloe said, smiling. She pretended to shiver. *Hmmm . . . ,* Sam thought. Interesting. Not a bubblehead.

"Hey, you know what's on now?" she told him, looking at her watch. "My favorite old cartoon—*Bugs Bunny!*"

Sam's opinion of this girl was rising with every word she said. Any girl who liked Bugs had to be an okay person. "Sorry, kid, Bugs is cool, but the Road Runner's on next."

She grabbed for the remote. He held it at arm's length from her. "Excuse me? Whose house is this anyway?" he asked with a grin. "And let's not forget you're just a lowly freshman. You get no say."

"Ah, but I'm the guest," she challenged, reaching for the remote again. She giggled, and he noticed how warm those light blue eyes of hers were. He had a good feeling about this girl.

She got ahold of the end of the remote and tried to tug it away. He held firm, aware he was grinning. God, it felt good to have Elizabeth off his mind for a second. He grabbed the remote away. "Aha!" he said. "You'll never get it!" He waved it under her nose.

Each time she strained and grabbed, he yanked it just out of her reach. Chloe was cute and fun, and normally he'd be flirting back with her in a more sexual way, even though he wasn't really interested. But with this one he'd better be careful. She was Jessica's friend, which meant she'd probably be hanging around the house a lot. That could get sticky if she really started liking him and expected something more from him. And she was just a freshman, so unless Sam wanted to be the one who introduced Chloe to post-high-school heartbreak, he'd better back off.

She tried to grab the remote, pressing every inch of her T-shirt against his back. If he wasn't sure before if she was just being playful or really flirting, he knew now. *Careful, Sam,* he told himself. As he tried to wrestle away, she tightened her grip around his chest with her arms, reaching. She tickled him, which made him laugh. Tickled him more. And more. "Stop . . . Chloe . . . I can't take it!" he sputtered between laughs. She started laughing too, tickling him harder.

"Glad to see you haven't been sitting around worrying about me."

He turned around to see Elizabeth glaring at

him from the doorway. Neil nodded at Chloe and headed upstairs. Chloe let go of the remote and scooted over on the sofa.

"So how's your hand?" Sam asked Elizabeth. "Did you need stitches?"

"Like you care," she muttered.

"You must be Jessica's twin sister!" Chloe exclaimed, jumping up from the sofa. "It's amazing how identical you guys are! I know Jess from art history, and we ran into each other at the library, and she's gonna take me over to Theta house after she's done upstairs; isn't that great of her? I'm a freshman, and I'm dying to join Theta, and—wow, I can't believe how identical you two are—I mean it's, like, amazing! Ohmigod—I'm babbling on and on and I just realized your hand is all bandaged up—what happened—are you okay?"

Elizabeth was staring openmouthed at Chloe, and Sam couldn't suppress his amusement. Elizabeth had on that awkward smile she got whenever she didn't know what to say. He knew exactly what Elizabeth was thinking. That was the curse and the blessing of their *housemateship* since he'd never call what they were *friends*. She was thinking that Chloe seemed way too young for him.

"Nice to meet you, Chloe," Elizabeth said. "So Jessica's upstairs?"

"She's just changing her clothes before we go

to Theta house," Chloe replied. "She told Sam not to scare me away and to be nice and polite—isn't that so funny? I mean, Sam seems like one of the nicest and most polite guys I've met so far!"

"Key word there is *seems,* Chloe," Elizabeth said, narrowing her eyes at Sam. She smiled at Chloe, then headed upstairs.

Sam had had every intention of apologizing profusely to Elizabeth when she got home. But of course, she had to act like Ms. Superiority and put him in his place. He was glad she hadn't given him the chance. The bigger a jerk she thought he was, the more she'd keep her distance. Of all the girls in this world, why did it have to be Elizabeth Wakefield who he had this weird connection with?

"Wow," Chloe said when they heard the sound of a door slamming from up the stairs. "She and Jessica are like identical *looking* but *way* different in personality." She moved close to Sam and leaned over to whisper in his ear, "It's *Elizabeth* who Jessica should have told not to scare me!"

Sam laughed. "You just earned yourself Bugs," he said, handing her the prized remote control.

Chapter Six

"Enough, enough, enough!" Professor Prichard yelled. "Violas, passable. Violins, you are too jerky. Cellos, are you trying to give me a headache?" He ran his hand through his white mane of hair. "You," he said, pointing his baton right at Dana. "You must keep your wrist perpendicular to the fingerboard as you ascend, even if you have to adjust your entire body position."

Dana blinked against the tears that were forming. How dare he treat her like a novice! She had been playing the cello since she was eight. She *knew* how to hold her hands.

"Take it from the beginning—again," he commanded. Amid the sound of music books flipping back to the start of the piece, Professor Prichard lifted his baton and counted off the beat.

As they played, sweat popped out across Dana's

forehead and upper lip. She had never worked so hard before, and yet nothing she did was right. Her hands were shaking so badly that twice she nearly dropped her bow. Beside her Becky was sawing away, hitting every note perfectly.

"Stop! Stop!" The professor hit his baton against the stand so hard that a chunk of it went flying across the room. He threw the remaining piece over one shoulder and stomped over to the cabinet for a new one. "Again!" he ordered, climbing back onto his carpeted block of wood and lifting his new baton. "I know we are over time, but we will start again and again and again until you people get this right!"

Dana had lost count of just how many times they had started the *pezzo capriccioso*. And it seemed each time it got faster and harder. The professor was waving his baton as if he were swatting at a swarm of flies. On and on and on they played until she thought she would die from exhaustion.

Finally he announced that they were finished for the day. Sighing with relief, Dana began gathering up her music. Her back and arms ached. Her head ached. Her fingers were numb. She glanced at her watch and groaned. *Great—now I don't even have time to take my cello back to my car.* She was going to have drag it all the way across campus to the language-arts building. Becky tapped her on the shoulder. "I'm going to practice for a few hours this afternoon at my garage studio—wanna come?"

Dana snapped the lid on her cello case and hefted it to her chair. "Are you *kidding?*" she asked, staring at the girl.

"If you don't want to, just say so, Dana," Becky snapped, glaring at her. "But by not practicing, you're affecting the *whole* class. And that means more killer classes like this one."

Can my life get any lower than this? Dana asked herself. A *freshman* was insinuating—no, flat-out *saying*—that *she* needed to practice. That *she* was holding up the class. Obviously it wasn't bad enough that Dana had suffered through yet another grueling, embarrassing mixed-strings class. No, now a freshman bitch felt the need to show Dana up. All week she'd put up with the perfect Becky.

She snatched up the rest of her music. "Thanks *anyway,* Becky, but I've got a class in fifteen minutes, and then, well, it's Friday, and I do have a *life.* I'm really sorry if you *don't.*"

Dana realized she was shouting. And that her voice was the only one in the room. Everyone was staring at her. Dana felt her face burning red. Felt the tears stinging her eyes. Saw Becky looking at her with a mixture of pity and disgust. Pity, for Dana Upshaw—who used to be the most promising cello player at SVU.

Dana grabbed her cello and lumbered out of the room. *Maybe I should just go home,* she thought. She hadn't read the assigned chapters for her lit class anyway, which meant she couldn't even follow along. And she didn't need another professor giving her disapproving looks for not doing her homework.

But last night had been worth not practicing, not studying.

Last night she and Todd had celebrated. Big time. And everything was great between them again. They'd finally celebrated the job Todd had gotten a few days ago as a bar back at some new club that recently opened. She'd been less than thrilled when he'd come home exuberant that night with the news. Her reaction had caused another argument, but last night she'd finally apologized and congratulated him, and he'd melted.

Dana still wasn't thrilled that he'd be spending many late nights away from her. But Todd was so sweet about the whole thing. He'd told her that all he wanted was to be able to take care of her— the love of his life. That the bar was just a few miles from their apartment, that she could come hang out there anytime.

That had made her feel better, but she still didn't like that his having a job, especially at night, would cut into their time together. She barely saw

him as it was. And she didn't like that he'd be surrounded by women at this bar. At least it wasn't
an SVU hangout, she thought. Todd had described it as a "townie" bar, where people who
lived and worked in the neighborhood went.
She'd been relieved to hear that; it wasn't like
Todd had anything in common with people who
weren't in college and had full-time jobs.

As Dana cut across the quad and thought more
about last night, her mood perked up a little. *So I
didn't do my lit homework,* she thought. *I can still
go to class and listen. No one says I have to partici-
pate. It's not playing the cello.*

Dana only had five minutes to get to the
language-arts building. With her cello clunking
against her legs and the guy in front of her walking like a snail, she'd be unprepared and *late.*
"Excuse me," she said, trying to slip in front of
the guy on the path. He had on an SVU football
jacket. Figured. Football players acted like they
owned the school. It was no wonder he was walking so slowly and taking up the whole path.

As she passed him, her cello hit him. "Hey!" he
called out.

Too bad, Mr. BMOC. I'm sure you'll live.

"Hey, Dana! Wait up!"

Huh? He knew her? She turned around, and
her mouth dropped open. *Tom Watts.* She

couldn't believe it. Tom Watts, looking better than ever, really muscular, and totally unstressed, stood before her in an SVU *football* jacket.

"So you're back on the team?" she asked, stunned. Back when she and Tom had had their little torrid affair last year, he'd been SVU's ex-star-quarterback-turned-dedicated-journalist. He'd worked at the campus television station day and night. She'd been amazed he'd had time to have a relationship with her. If you could even call it a relationship. He'd been on the rebound from Miss High and Mighty, Queen Elizabeth Wakefield. And then he'd gone right back to her, breaking Dana's heart.

She'd really loved Tom. But she thanked her lucky stars that he'd dumped her. Because then she'd met Todd—her one true love. That Todd was also an ex-boyfriend of Elizabeth's was something Dana liked to forget. Though Elizabeth had great taste in guys, Dana had no idea what either Tom or Todd had seen in prissy Elizabeth.

Dana set her heavy cello case on the ground.

"Yup," he said, smiling. "And I'm loving it. I can't believe how much I've missed it. Hey, so how's SVU's star cellist doing?"

She shrugged. "Okay," she said. "Maybe not so great."

"With the cello?" he asked. "Or with other stuff?" Tom seemed really concerned. Whenever anyone asked how she was, they usually wanted to hear "fine," "how are you," "great," "see ya." But Tom wasn't saying, "Oh, too bad, well, gotta run," and taking off. He was looking at her with genuine concern in his eyes.

Wow, Dana thought. *It's not like SVU's star quarterback didn't have anything better to do than listen to her sob stories. Maybe he's still the same old Tom—a really good listener.*

"Everything," she said, relieved to vent a little. "Well, I shouldn't say *everything,* actually," she amended. "Things with Todd are great, but I don't know. . . . It's really hard sometimes, living together in our own apartment, dealing with everything ourselves, not having any time. You know. But the cello—forget it. It's like I've lost it; all my talent is just, like, gone."

"Dana, you can't mean that," he said. "From what you just said, it sounds like you're adjusting to a lot of new stuff—new school year, new living arrangements. Things will even out. Cut yourself a break."

"I tried that," she told him. "I really have. But every music class is worse than the last. What's really weird is that I'm fine when I'm practicing at home or playing for Todd. It's only in classes that I totally suck."

"So maybe you're just getting used to being back in school," Tom pointed out. "Maybe you could try to pretend you're home, playing for Todd or something, the next time you're in class."

"I've tried that too," Dana said, which was true. She'd tried everything. "I'm worried that maybe I just don't belong in school anymore, you know?"

"I sort of *do* know, Dana," he told her. "Not about cello, but you can imagine how weird it was for me to realize that being Tom Watts, superjournalist, didn't fit me anymore. I know what it's like to have your world not feel right. Like there's something else you're meant to do. For me it was rejoining the team. Expressing myself physically instead of intellectually."

Dana felt tears forming—not because she was upset, but because for the first time in weeks she felt understood. Validated. "Tom, you don't know how much better I feel just having someone to talk to about this, someone who understands—"

"Can't you talk to Todd?" he asked. "He *is* your boyfriend."

"I've tried, but I guess it's harder for him to understand because he hasn't been through it, you know?" Dana poked at a rock with her foot. "It's really not his fault—and he is a great boyfriend. I don't know. I *do* know that he'd freak if I told him I was having all these thoughts about dropping out for this semester."

"Dana, it is your decision, your life," Tom said.

"I'm sure Todd will support your decision. If he doesn't, then, well, that says something too."

"I know you're right," she replied. "But Todd feels like he can do it all, so he figures that I'll feel that way too. Now that he has a job too, it's like I'll never see him. If I take the semester off, at least I can figure things out and have time with him too."

"Mr. BMW got a job?" Tom laughed. "Very impressive."

"He's a bar back at Frankie's—a new club that just opened in our neighborhood."

"Wait a minute," Tom said. "Todd Wilkins, with his trust fund, is working as a busboy at a townie bar?"

Dana was about to tell Tom to stop ragging on Todd when a gigantic football player charged into him, sending him stumbling into Dana. "Guard up, Wildman!"

Another guy, even bigger, was right behind him. "Hey, Wildman, we're headed over to Sigma house. C'mon, the party can't get started without you."

Tom turned back to Dana. "Trust me. Everything will be okay," he told her. "You'll figure it out." He squeezed her hand and headed off with his friends.

She looked across the quad at the clock tower. Her lit class had started ten minutes ago.

She picked up her cello case, turned around, and headed toward the commuter parking lot. The only place she wanted to be was home. If she could talk to Tom about how she felt, then she could certainly talk to Todd, her own boyfriend. She just had to make him understand, that's all. Once he really understood how she felt, he'd be able to help her get back on track, if not with the cello, then something else.

Dana realized that from the way Tom had talked about Todd and his BMW and his bank account, Tom didn't know the first thing about her incredible boyfriend. Todd was taking care of the two of them himself, not with a free ride. It was Todd she should be talking to, her wonderful Todd.

He was all that mattered to her anymore anyway.

Jessica double-checked her knapsack to make sure she had everything she'd need for her lit and Spanish classes: textbooks, pencils, pens, highlighter, notebooks, change for the copy machine, perfume . . . just in case she should run into Tristan.

For the first time in her entire life, she wished it were Monday. She wished she could go to sleep tonight and have it be Monday when she woke up. Who needed a weekend when she had to wait until Monday morning to finally be alone with Tristan

Patterson? She recalled how he glanced at her yesterday in the discussion section. Not a flirtatious glance, not an admiring glance—just an ordinary glance.

Is he interested and acting professional in class, or is he not interested and making that clear? she wondered for the thousandth time. Why couldn't she tell? She'd wanted to pick Alejandro's brain some more after class, but he'd hurried off somewhere.

She slung her knapsack over her shoulder and pulled open the front door—to see Chloe Murphy poised to knock. "Hey, Chloe," she said. "I wish I'd known you were coming by—I've got two back-to-back classes."

"Oh, you do?" Chloe replied. "I was really hoping we could hang out and talk about Theta." Chloe looked totally bummed. "Visiting Theta house the other day was so great! I can't thank you enough for that. It's too bad Lila wasn't there—I'd love to see her again. And your other friends—maybe you could bring me by another time and introduce me? I'd love to meet them."

"No problem, Chloe," Jessica told her. She heard a loud crash and turned around. "Sam! If you're leaving a mess of dishes in the sink again, you'd better wash them, now!"

"Oh, Sam's home, great!" Chloe said, stepping around Jessica into the living room. "Since I walked all the way here, maybe I'll just hang out with him for a little while. That way it's not a wasted trip. Sam and I are both cartoon fans."

Jessica saw Sam come out of the kitchen with a giant-sized sub and a two-liter bottle of Gatorade. Like Sam ever exerted himself to need a sports drink, she thought.

"Hi, Chloe," Sam said. "Just in time for Bugs Bunny and one bite of my sandwich, if you behave yourself." He grinned at her. Jessica rolled her eyes. It was nice of Sam to be pleasant to Chloe, considering that he was so obnoxious to his own housemates. But she could tell by the way Chloe's eyes lit up that Chloe liked Sam, big time. *If he hurts her, he's dead meat,* she vowed.

"Okay, well, Chloe, maybe I'll see you later if you're still here," Jessica said. "Have fun," she whispered, giving Chloe a wink.

As Jessica walked down the street, she realized how alike she and Chloe were. Or how like Chloe she *used* to be. Chloe knew what she wanted, and she was going after it: Theta, a friendship with Jessica, *Sam.* . . . She had to give the girl credit. But Jessica was also worried about her. Chloe was impulsive, just like Jessica was trying so hard *not* to be. Being impulsive, acting before you really *thought,* could get you into trouble. But Chloe would have to learn that for herself, maybe the hard way, just like Jessica had learned it. Impulsive people didn't take advice that didn't appeal to them.

Elizabeth had come running into Jessica's room the other day to tell her she'd better warn her friend about Sam. But who's to say that Sam and Chloe weren't a good match or that he didn't really like her? What made Elizabeth so sure that Sam Burgess couldn't possibly fall in love? Elizabeth hadn't liked Jessica's words of wisdom.

Sometimes Jessica was convinced that Sam and Elizabeth were madly in love but that neither of them knew it. The way they snarled at each other every second meant *something*. And sometimes Jessica would catch a glance one gave the other when both thought no one was watching them. It was a glance that had longing in it, admiration, respect, wonder. And then it would be gone, replaced by the glares Sam and Elizabeth loved to give each other. Maybe Jessica was wrong—maybe they totally hated each other.

I'd better pick up on how to read people and their body language, she thought as Tristan's face floated into her mind.

"Dana?" Todd whispered. "Are you okay? Are you sick?" He'd just gotten home, psyched that it was Friday night, only to find Dana in bed with the blankets over her head. He pulled off his sweatshirt and opened the closet to find a cool shirt to change into for work. He couldn't wait to go to Frankie's.

She peeked out from the covers. "Hi, Todd. Are you changing for work? It's not close to six already, is it?" She bolted up.

"It's five," he told her, taking a black T-shirt from his drawer in the dresser. "Have you been asleep for a while? I thought you had classes till six."

"I went to mixed strings, but then I just came home. I skipped lit and music theory. I had the worst day—it was so bad in strings—everything is so bad—"

Dana's eyes were all puffy. He sat down on the edge of the bed and took her hand. "Dana— what's wrong? What are you talking about?"

She looked at him and chewed on her lip.

"What was so bad?" he asked. "Did something happen?"

"I totally screwed up in strings—a girl in my class, a *freshman,* told me I'd better start practicing more, that I was holding back the whole class." Todd could see the tears pooling in Dana's eyes.

"Dana, come here," he said, pulling her into a hug. "Look, it's okay. You had a bad day, that's all. It's like when I was on the basketball team and missed some really important shots. I screwed up, and the whole team was affected. But then the next day I was fine and shooting great."

"Thanks for agreeing that I must be screwing up

and messing things up for everyone!" she snapped.

Todd sighed. He didn't have the energy for this right now. He'd had back-to-back classes all day, and all he wanted was to chow down on something really good for dinner, watch the rest of the baseball game on TV, and hang out until he had to leave for work. He'd expected to come home and spend some time with Dana. But she was all freaked out over a stupid class.

"I'm not saying that," he told her. "I'm just saying I'm sure you'll be fine Monday. The Dana Upshaw I know and love isn't a crybaby. She doesn't get squashed because her professor yells at her or some idiot freshman makes a jealous comment. Right?"

He'd noticed Dana stiffen at the word *crybaby*. Was he being too harsh with her? *Am I supposed to listen and nod and tell her I understand, you poor baby, everyone's so mean, you just drop that nasty class?*

He squeezed her hand. He didn't know what he was supposed to say. He did know that he felt like picking up an overstuffed pastrami sandwich and a big bag of potato chips from the deli near Frankie's and then hanging out with Rita, who always opened up at three o'clock to set up.

Rita was so cool and wise. She talked about things he'd never heard anyone talk about, at least not the way Rita did. She spoke about dreams— ones that were actually possible if you worked for them. Rita wanted to buy Frankie's one day and expand it into a bigger nightclub, with restaurant service and a maitre d'. She spoke about it so passionately. Anytime there was a problem with a shipment or someone calling in sick, she didn't freak out and run home under the covers. She dealt with it because she had a vision for her future. She used that word a lot—*vision*. Todd liked it.

"Todd, you're not even listening to me," Dana said.

She was right. Dana was standing right in front of him, waving her hand in front of his eyes. He looked at her, his beautiful Dana, with her big hazel eyes and her long, brown, curly hair. She really was so beautiful.

And he was such a jerk. The woman he loved was having a problem, and all he could do was think she was being a baby. She needed his support, not his condemnation. Dana wasn't Rita—who was like thirty years old. Dana was just a nineteen-year-old college student.

"Dana," he murmured, wrapping his arms around her. He might not know exactly what to say to make her feel better about her class, but he did know how to make Dana Upshaw break out in a smile. "Why don't we whip up something for dinner together and set it out like a picnic in the living room, with a candle and our one wineglass and everything? And then we'll have each other for dessert. . . . "

Dana looked at him and grinned, and he felt much better. "I love you, Todd," she said, tilting her head and kissing him.

"I love you too," he told her. *I just wish I understood you.*

Elizabeth poked at the edges of her bandage out of sheer boredom. She picked up the campus newspaper and thumbed through the activities section—there had to be something interesting going on this Friday night. Although living off campus had its advantages, it had its drawbacks too. Namely: isolation.

Elizabeth had her housemates, but their schedules were wildly different, so they weren't often home at the same time. And it wasn't like she could walk out of her room and down the hall into a lounge full of students hanging out. The library wasn't just steps away anymore, nor was the coffee bar or student center. Campus life seemed so far away. It was like she wasn't really a part of it anymore. Not in the same way.

She'd called Nina twice tonight but got her answering machine. *At least Nina's out having a life,* she thought. *Even if she's only in the library studying.*

The phone rang, and Elizabeth snatched it. "Nina?" she asked, already anticipating the hamburger she'd order at the coffee shop.

"Elizabeth?" asked a very sexy male voice.

Ohmigod. *Finn!* She couldn't believe he'd really called!

"Hello?" he asked.

"Hi, uh, sorry," she said. "I thought you were someone else. This is Elizabeth—who's this?" she asked, knowing full well it was him.

"It's Finn Robinson—we met in the ER a couple of days ago?"

"Finn, hi!" she said. Her hand was trembling. "How are you?"

"Doing great," he replied. "I was calling to find out the same thing about you."

Oh. Elizabeth deflated. He'd meant what he said about wanting her number so he could call to check on her hand.

"That's really thoughtful of you," she told him. It was, actually. "I'm doing really well—my hand doesn't hurt anymore at all."

"Good," he said. "Especially because that might mean you'll feel up to having dinner next Friday?"

Elizabeth felt her entire face light up.

"Next Friday?" she repeated like an idiot.

"I know it's an entire week away," he said, "but I'm booked up with my study groups till then. Med school is pretty intense."

"Oh, no, I mean, next Friday is fine. I've got a really busy week too." She grabbed the campus

110

newspaper and rustled some pages near the receiver. "Yup, I'm just flipping through my day planner, and I'm not free till Thursday. I even double booked Wednesday!"

Yeah. To study for journalism and *Western civilization.* But she had to sound busy, like she had a life. Not like she was sitting around her room with nothing to do on a Friday.

"You like Cajun food?" he asked. "A great new place just opened not too far away."

"I don't think I've ever had it," she told him. This was so exciting! Dating a sophisticated older guy like Finn meant lots of new experiences would be coming her way. She would be introduced to new exotic cuisines, new interests, new ways of looking at things, new everything!

"It's really hot and spicy," he added. "Maybe we should stick to Chinese or Italian?"

"No, let's go with Cajun," she said. "Hot and spicy and different sounds great."

"Then hot and spicy, it is," he replied. "I'll pick you up at seven?"

"Seven," she agreed. She gave him directions to the duplex, and after telling her he was really looking forward to it, they hung up.

Elizabeth rushed downstairs to tell Jessica. She burst into her sister's room, but Jessica wasn't in there.

Elizabeth could hear voices coming from

downstairs, but because Sam's stereo was blaring as usual, she couldn't tell if the girl's laughter she just caught was Jessica's or Sam's new constant guest, Chloe. She was dying to tell her sister about Finn—if there was one thing Jessica appreciated, it was news of a hot date, especially with someone like Finn Robinson.

She heard giggles coming from the living room. Girly giggles. Even Jessica had stopped that idiotic kind of flirting in seventh grade. "Sam!" she heard the girl's voice shriek. Giggle. Giggle.

Just as Elizabeth came downstairs into the living room, a head of red hair popped up over the back the couch. *Chloe.* Apparently, from Chloe's position and Elizabeth's inability to see Sam, Chloe and Sam had been lying down on the sofa.

Elizabeth twisted around as quietly as she could to slip back up the stairs. "Elizabeth, hi!" Chloe called out. Elizabeth turned back around. Chloe had a big smile on her face. "Sam and I are watching the greatest old movie. Want some popcorn?"

"Uh, no, thanks," Elizabeth said.

Sam sat up, and Elizabeth could tell by his mussed sandy brown hair and Chloe's flushed face that the two of them had been doing more than just watching the greatest old movie.

"Chloe, hit pause," Sam said, standing up and stretching. "I'm gonna nuke up more popcorn and get more soda." *You mean make more of* Neil's *popcorn and get more of* my *Dr Pepper.*

As Sam passed Elizabeth on his way into the kitchen, he winked at her. "I'll replace your soda, Wakefield."

Elizabeth gave him a tight smile. "Do that," she said.

Sam disappeared behind the swinging door. Chloe was cracking up over a fast-food commercial. And Elizabeth was left to wonder what Sam's game was.

Was he working on Chloe to take advantage of her naiveté? It wasn't like he had to move a muscle to have a relationship with the girl. *She* was coming to *him.* As Jessica's friend, Chloe would naturally be around the house. He wouldn't have to take her out on dates, go to see her, or do anything other than exactly what he was doing: watching free movies on TV, eating everyone else's food, and making out on the sofa. And his bedroom was mere steps away. What more could Sam Burgess possibly want?

The worst thing Elizabeth could say about Chloe was that she seemed immature and tried too hard; otherwise, the girl seemed really nice and friendly. And she was Jessica's friend. The idea of Sam using Chloe until he got tired of her or until she wanted more from him . . .

"Chloe?" Elizabeth called out. Chloe's face

popped up over the back of the sofa. "Is Jessica in the bathroom or something?"

"No, she's not back from campus yet," Chloe said. "She was leaving as I arrived here—that was, like, hours ago. Hey, are you in Theta too?"

Elizabeth laughed. "No. Sororities are Jessica's department."

"What's yours?" Chloe asked.

Good question, Elizabeth thought. She moved over to the edge of the sofa and sat on the arm. "I'm not too sure anymore, actually," she told Chloe. "If you'd asked me that last year, I would have said journalism in a heartbeat. Being a reporter. But now I'm expanding my options."

"So you have no idea, huh?" Chloe said.

Elizabeth smiled, but felt the sting. "Guess not," she replied. "But that's okay. I don't think any nineteen-year-old is supposed to know what she wants to do with the rest of her life."

"Well, I'm only eighteen, so I guess it's okay that I only know what I want to do *tonight,*" Chloe said, laughing. "Sam is soooo cute, isn't he? You're all so lucky that you live here. I can't wait to tell all my friends in Oakley that I'm hanging out with a bunch of sophomores in your off-campus house—"

A glass shattered in the kitchen, followed by a string of curses. *That better not be one of my glasses. . . .* "I'll see you later, Chloe," Elizabeth said, hopping up and heading for the stairs. "If Jess comes home, will you tell her to come up to my room?"

Chloe nodded and ran into the kitchen. *Crunch. Crunch. Giggle. Giggle.* Elizabeth heard the swinging doors swoosh open and Chloe calling out, "Hey, Elizabeth, do you know where you guys keep the broom and dustpan?"

"Tell Sam to use his hands," she called back from the second-floor landing.

"You are *so* strong!" Annie exclaimed as Todd lifted two racks of clean glasses over to the bar. Annie was one of the waitresses. She looked a little like Dana, with her long, curly hair. But she was older, maybe twenty-two.

"And cute too," Cathy, the bartender, added. "Here, Todd. Your cut of our tips." She slid a fistful of bills across the bar. "You're doing a great job here," she told him. She poured him a Coke from the soda fountain and handed it to him.

Todd took a sip, sighed, and sat down on a bar stool with the letter *R* painted on it. "When I start acting really conceited, it's your fault," he told them, laughing. He glanced at his watch—he couldn't believe it was two-twenty in the morning already.

Annie smiled. "At my last job the bar backs were so lazy. If the tables don't get cleared of empty glasses and bottles, the people get pissed off and it

115

affects my tips. Which affects your cut," she said.

"Ryan," Cathy called out. The DJ looked over from where he was putting away CDs in his little booth. "Put on something good. I'm in the mood to dance."

A great song came on, and Cathy came around the bar and grabbed Annie with one hand and Todd with the other. Cathy and Annie started dancing right there, on the small dance floor in front of the bar. "Come on, Todd," Cathy said. "Shake it."

"Is it okay?" he asked, looking around for Rita. "I mean, I know it's past two and we're closed, but shouldn't I be finishing up in the back?"

"I heard that, Wilkins," said Rita, who pushed through the double doors behind the bar. "You're a good kid. I knew I should have hired you," she added with a smile. "The back is as spotless as it's gonna get. Hey, I need to be here for about another hour to finish receipts. Anyone want to hang around for Chinese on me?"

"Steamed veggie dumplings and a side of fried rice," Ryan called out.

As Annie, Cathy, and Todd told Rita their orders, all the while continuing to dance, Todd actually pinched himself on the arm. *This has to be a dream,* he thought. *No way am I having this much fun at work.*

Ryan came over to join them, and the four of them danced together, lost in the music, in knowing their shifts were over, in the anticipation of moo goo gai pan.

"Hey, Todd, I'll make you a deal," Ryan said. "I'll take you to this amazing after-hours club that just opened on Sky Drive if you let me drive the Beemer."

"Deal!" Todd agreed. "But I can't stay too long. I told my girlfriend I'd be home around three, so maybe just for a half hour."

"I'd call the wife and tell her you'll be home around five if I were you, Todd," Annie said. "Ryan's a total party boy."

Dana was probably asleep right now anyway, Todd realized. So what was the difference, then, if he got home at three or five?

Todd grinned. "After we stuff ourselves with moo goo, we're there!"

Chapter
Seven

Jessica stood in front of the mirror in the arts building rest room and blotted her lipstick. She wanted to look good but natural, like she wasn't putting on makeup to be tutored. She smoothed her shiny blond hair, checked her teeth for any signs of the cinnamon-raisin bagel she'd had for breakfast, and then popped a Certs in her mouth.

Pulling a tiny piece of white lint off her cropped black cardigan, Jessica looked in the mirror. *Deep breath, deep breath,* she told herself. *I'm a nervous wreck,* she realized. *Over a guy!* But then again, Tristan Patterson wasn't just a guy. He was *the* guy.

She glanced at her watch—9:59. Time to go. Time to have Tristan to herself for an entire hour.

She left the rest room and walked down the hall to Tristan's office. *Deep breath, deep breath.*

She knocked, her excitement over seeing him again almost overwhelming.

"Come on in—it's open," she heard him call out. "Jessica, right on time," Tristan said, standing up behind his desk.

The sight of him made her knees feel weak. His smile almost did her in. "Have a seat on the sofa," he said, gesturing at the two-person love seat.

Jessica was grateful to sit down and control her wobbly knees. She anticipated the feel of him sitting so close beside her. As he walked over to her, she felt his presence so acutely, it almost freaked her out. She was overwhelmed by the thought of what it would be like to kiss him, to feel those incredible arms around her, his hand running through her hair. . . .

He sat down on the arm of the love seat—on the side farthest from her. She felt a mixture of disappointment and relief. On the one hand, she wanted him squeezed right next to her, but on the other, it made her a little nervous too.

"So," he began, opening the textbook. "I think the best approach is for us to meet weekly for a few weeks." *You are so gorgeous,* she thought, then realized she was staring. She darted her eyes back to her own textbook and opened it to the page he was on. "In each session," he continued, "we'll go over the entire week's lecture and discussion sections. Then after a few weeks of tutoring, we'll see how you're doing, if you feel caught up enough to go it alone."

If he noticed that her eyes drifted to his and held for a bit too long, he didn't miss a beat in what he was saying. *Maybe he's not interested?* she wondered again, feeling a little deflated. Maybe grad students looked at undergrads the way high schoolers looked at junior high schoolers: like kids.

Maybe . . . *maybe* she should concentrate on her tutoring session, she told herself. It wasn't like she was here solely because she had the major hots for her TA. She *did* want help in grasping some of the concepts they'd learned so far in class. Art history *did* mean something to her.

But so did having Tristan ask her out.

He pulled a picture out of a manila envelope. "Do you recognize this?" he asked.

"Yes!" she said. "That's the *Temptation*." She almost couldn't believe she knew it. She tried to recall the painter, then shook her head. "I can't seem to remember who painted it, though," she admitted, embarrassed. She didn't want Tristan to think she was a dope who didn't know *anything*.

"Masolino," Tristan told her. "But don't be too hard on yourself, Jessica. I don't expect you to know all the names of all the paintings or the artists." He smiled at her frown. "You'll eventually be able to name them all. What's important right now is that you begin to get used to *analyzing* what you see. Look at the picture, and tell me what you see."

"I see a naked man and woman—," Jessica began, then got embarrassed again. She sounded like an idiot. A five-year-old would have given the same answer!

"Go on, Jessica," Tristan told her. "Be very specific about what you see and what you think you see."

"And I see a snake, with a human head," she said, staring at the painting. She tilted her head to the left, then to the right. Suddenly she realized what she was looking at, and excitement rushed over her. "It's Adam and Eve, isn't it?" she asked, looking up at Tristan. "And that's the serpent, right?"

"Excellent, Jessica!" Tristan exclaimed. "Go on. Tell me the specifics of what you see."

His praise stirred something in her, made her feel . . . *smart*. Jessica Wakefield, intelligently discussing art? Unbelievable. But that was exactly what she was doing.

"The man, Adam, has half a beard, sort of like yours. But his wasn't too thick, either," she added, laughing. Tristan grinned. "And Eve has blond hair—"

"A lot like yours," Tristan interjected, and she noticed his gaze drifting over her hair, then back to her eyes. *He's checking me out,* she thought.

Maybe he seemed uninterested before because he thought I was a total airhead. And now that he sees I'm serious. . . . "So now," he continued. "Keeping in mind elements such as color, composition, texture, and movement, describe what this painting makes you *feel*."

Jessica squinted in concentration. She didn't want to say the wrong thing.

"Remember, Jessica, there's no wrong or right answer," he told her, as if he sensed she was nervous. "It's all a matter of developing your eye to notice what you might not have before." His words gave her the courage to tell the truth.

"Well, I feel like yelling at them, at Adam and Eve, I mean," Jessica said, looking back and forth from the painting to Tristan. "They seem so out of it, just floating there, totally unaware that the snake is about to ruin their lives. You know," she added, "it's almost like the lack of color in the painting matches how blasé they seem."

"Jessica, that's really terrific!" he praised. "Your interpretation is excellent."

Jessica beamed. *Terrific, excellent.* It was like he was giving her an A-plus as a tutee.

As he discussed realistic flesh tones and formal expressions and detachment, Jessica found herself listening with the rapt attention she'd usually reserve for good gossip at Theta house. "So now let's move on to this one." He pulled another picture from the folder.

Jessica stared at the painting. "There's a glare coming from the window," she said. "Can you angle it a bit?"

Tristan slid down onto the cushion so that he was sitting right next to her. Their thighs almost touched. Her toes tingled.

"Do you recognize this?" he asked her. When she shook her head, this time without any sense of embarrassment, he told her it was *Expulsion*, by Masaccio. "Done at the same time as the *Temptation*, for the same chapel."

"This one is scary," she said, studying the card.

"Exactly," he agreed. "Why?"

"It's not as smooth, and the faces are blurry."

"What you're describing is the artist's style," he said. "Very good."

Jessica Wakefield was describing an artist's style. Again a rush of pride came over her. She had no idea she knew how to do that! "But it's kind of funny," she went on. "Well, not funny, but Eve is covering her nakedness with her hands, like she's ashamed, and Adam is just covering his face, like he's afraid."

"Jessica, I'm really impressed," Tristan said, laying the card down on his lap. He turned to face her, and they were so close that it would require absolutely no movement to kiss him. "You have an excellent eye. Developing that eye is what's key."

Now she absolutely wanted to kiss him. No one had ever said those kinds of things to her before. No one had ever made her feel smart or told her she had an excellent eye.

He slid the card into the folder and extracted another one. "Now look at this sculpture by Rodin, aptly titled *The Kiss*. It's one of my favorites."

One of his favorites. There was instantly something more special about it because of that. She took the picture from Tristan's hands and held it closer. "I think it's amazing how someone can take a big hunk of stone and turn it into something so lifelike. I mean, it's almost embarrassing, like we're spying on two real lovers. Their passion practically oozes off this page."

"The sensuality is what I like most about baroque art," he said, angling his head close to hers to look at the card she held. "And excellent again, Jessica, that you recognized it in the sculpture."

Kiss me, kiss me, kiss me. . . . She turned her head to face him, and for a second he looked into her eyes, then back at the card. She felt his fingers brush against hers. She closed her eyes, waiting to feel the pressure of his warm hand on hers, the pressure of his hot lips on her own. But all she felt was Tristan getting up off the sofa.

As acutely as she'd felt his nearness, she felt the loss of it. Her eyes popped open. He was sliding the card back into the folder as he walked over to his desk. He dropped the folder on top of a stack, then started gathering some folders. She glanced at her watch. Wow—it was a little after eleven. How had an hour gone by so fast?

She'd give anything for him to sit back down and kiss her, gentle little kisses that would deepen and deepen and deepen. . . .

"Well, Jessica," he said, turning to look at her. "I don't even think you'll require more than one more tutoring session. As I've said, your eye is excellent, and once you build your confidence, look out!" He grinned, but the compliment and his faith in her were overshadowed by his obvious lack of romantic interest in her.

One more tutoring session—that's only one more hour together. Which means Tristan sees me as an eager student—that's all. If he was interested, he'd make sure they had *several* sessions lined up.

She grabbed her knapsack and slipped it over one shoulder as she stood up. "Tristan, thank you *so* much for today," she said, trying to sound more excited than she felt. "Is this time good for next week?"

"You know what?" he said, grabbing his day planner and flipping it open. "I get the sense you'll lose a bit of your fire with a week between sessions. I have a free hour and a half tomorrow at four. Can you make it?"

Now she didn't know what to think. But whether he was interested or not, he was making it clear that he cared about her as a student. He was so amazing! Gorgeous, brilliant, caring. Gorgeous . . .

This wasn't a lost cause. She had one more shot. An hour and a half tomorrow to get Tristan Patterson to ask her out. And she was going to take that shot big time.

"Tomorrow at four is perfect!"

If Sam didn't kiss her—on the lips—in the next thirty minutes, Chloe was just gonna grab him and plant one on him herself. She was snuggled against him on the sofa as they watched a video. Snuggled, like boyfriend-girlfriend. But no kisses, no touching, no nothing ever—like friends. This snuggling-buddies stuff was nice, really nice, actually, but Chloe needed Sam as a *boyfriend*.

Friends didn't cut it. Not if she was ever going to live down the Tom Watts disaster. Everyone on her floor at Oakley was calling her Cody in a singsong voice. Moira refused to call Chloe anything *but* Cody. All week Chloe had tried to explain that she hadn't meant to lie about her relationship with Tom, that the whole thing had just snowballed, that she'd really thought he'd felt more for her. That they should all be *sympathizing* with her broken heart instead of making fun of her.

But no one would even listen to her long enough to make all that sound believable. "*Whatever,* Cody," was the usual response.

So, to avoid Oakley for the weekend and to hang around with Sam and Jessica, Chloe had turned up at the duplex every day this past weekend, and she'd been welcomed, at least by Sam, since Jessica was never home. Sam would make the perfect new boyfriend. He might not be SVU's quarterback, an SVU student at all, for that matter, but he was incredibly good-looking and he was Jessica Wakefield's housemate. Jessica Wakefield's name carried a lot of weight around Oakley Hall, Chloe had noticed. She was a sophomore, she was a bigwig in Theta, and she had a lot of friends.

It was actually thanks to Jessica never being around that Chloe had managed to develop a fun friendship with Sam. And now it was time to turn that friendship into something more.

The only problem, aside from Sam not seeming at all interested in her that way, was that she wasn't exactly interested in him that way either. Despite how cute he was, how cool, how fun, and that he genuinely seemed to enjoy her company, Chloe wasn't really attracted to him. She liked him as a friend, which was exactly what he was, but not what she needed.

She thought about maybe just telling him her woes so he could help her out and *act* like her boyfriend for a few weeks around Oakley. But even with the guy in on it, a fake relationship was just too complicated.

No—she needed a real relationship. *And isn't friendship the perfect basis for a romantic relationship?* Chloe asked herself. She was sure that once she and Sam actually locked lips, they'd both see fireworks. That was it! They simply hadn't kissed, so they just didn't know that they were incredibly attracted to each other. Once they did, they'd be boyfriend-girlfriend for real, and Chloe would have the coolest boyfriend of anyone on this campus.

Finally relieved, Chloe sat up, grabbed the empty pretzel bowl, and headed into the kitchen. The three giant-sized bags of snacks she'd brought over were totally empty. Chloe checked the fridge—everything was weirdly marked with initials. Four yogurts had Post-it notes with the initials EW on them—Elizabeth. A half gallon of orange juice had an NM on it—Neil. A box of Chloe's favorite sugared cereal had a giant-sized JW on it—Jessica. Nothing in the fridge had Sam's initials, though.

As she stuffed their empty bags in the trash, she noticed the campus newspaper lying on the counter. Tom Watts's smiling face stared up at her from the front page in a football article.

Sam has *to become my boyfriend,* she told herself, scowling at Tom's photo.

"Chloe, hurry up, you're missing the best part," Sam called.

Chloe glanced at her watch. Ohmigod—if she didn't move her butt, she'd be late for political science.

She rushed into the living room and grabbed her knapsack. So much for Sam kissing her in the next thirty minutes or kissing him herself.

"Sam, I'm *so* late for poli sci—I've gotta go," she said, leaning over the back of the sofa to kiss him on the cheek. "I had such a blast!"

"You can't miss the end," he said, grabbing her shoulders and trying to pull her over onto the sofa.

"Get a room!" a guy's voice called out suddenly.

Chloe straightened up to see Neil grinning at her and Elizabeth glaring at Sam as they came through the front door into the living room.

"Chloe, have you actually met Neil?" Sam asked. "He's our other housemate. Neil, Chloe; Chloe, Neil."

"Nice to officially meet you, Neil," Chloe said, wondering how it was possible that Jessica and Elizabeth had managed to score two of the best-looking guys she'd ever seen as housemates. "Uh, hi, Elizabeth," she added before sprinting out.

Elizabeth doesn't like me, Chloe thought as she turned the corner. Then again, Elizabeth didn't seem to like anyone. Maybe she likes Sam herself? Nah. From what Chloe could tell, Sam and Elizabeth couldn't stand each other.

Which suited Chloe very well. Because with Elizabeth hating Sam and Jessica clearly not being into him *that way,* Chloe had zero competition—in that house, at least.

"Maybe we should start charging Chloe rent," Elizabeth said to Sam as she closed the door behind the sprinting redhead. Neil shot her a "that-was-bitchy" look as he rooted through the mail, but Elizabeth didn't care how she sounded. She cared about what like-'em-and-dump-'em Sam was doing to that freshman. "She was here practically all weekend."

"*Maybe* you should lighten up, Wakefield," Sam said. "*What* is your problem anyway?" He sat up on the sofa and stared at her.

What was *her* problem? Was he kidding? "*Maybe* I don't like watching guys like you lead on a sweet, innocent freshman who doesn't know better," Elizabeth replied. "*Maybe* I don't think you should be messing with Jessica's friend. Just because *you* don't care about anyone doesn't mean Jessica doesn't."

131

"*Maybe* I should head to the library for that nap I was planning to take," Neil cut in. "If the two of you are going to snap and snarl at each other all afternoon—*again*."

Elizabeth was about to turn to Neil to apologize, but Sam stood up and glared at her. "Go judge someone else, Elizabeth," he said. "Like you know anything about me," he added. "Maybe I *like* Chloe. Ever think of that?"

Actually, that possibility hadn't crossed her mind. But why would it? Sam had never showed an inkling of genuine like for anyone, even himself.

"I think I'll be taking that nap now," Neil said, rolling his eyes and leaving.

"And anyway," Sam continued as the door slammed behind Neil, " I'm not *leading* anyone on, not that it's any of your business in the first place. I'm not the one inviting Chloe over. She just turns up."

"Yeah, but you encourage her, Sam," Elizabeth countered. "'She just turns up,' but since Jessica hasn't been around, you so nicely decided to lounge on the sofa with Chloe all weekend and apparently half of today."

"*Exactly*, Liz," he said, sitting down and turning his attention to the television. "'*Lounge on the sofa.*' Which means we haven't been alone in my bedroom having wild sex, now, have we?" He turned to face her. "Why am I even defending myself to you?" He shook his head and stretched out, remote control in hand. "Wrestling's on, Liz. So enough."

"Sam, look—," she began, planning either to apologize or to say she'd mind her own business.

"No, *you* look, Elizabeth," he snapped, hitting the mute button. "I've said this before, and I'll say it a million times. You're a control freak. And it's showing, big time. You can't control other people, and you definitely can't control me." He hit the mute button again, and the wrestler's grunts were so loud, she could feel the vibration in her chest.

He lowered the volume and stared at her. "You know what I think, Wakefield?" he asked. "I think you're jealous."

Elizabeth stiffened. "Jealous of *what?*" she asked, feeling her face flush. "And *why,* pray tell?"

"You're jealous," he began, leaning back on the sofa and spreading his arms across the back, "because for the first time in the history of your control-freak life, *you* aren't involved with someone." He looked at the television, then back at her. "So you're jealous that a 'sweet, innocent freshman' managed to get something *you* can't."

Elizabeth's mouth dropped open, and her face burned. She took a deep breath.

"For your information, I happen to be *involved*

with a gorgeous med student. Who I happen to have a date with this Friday night. So you happen to be dead wrong, Sammy."

"Oooh, a med student!" he singsonged. "Whoo-hoo, Wakefield! That'll get you nothing but grief and maybe a ticket into Theta."

"Oh, now who's jealous?" she shot back. "What *that* will get me is a *real* relationship with a serious, ambitious, intelligent, and enlightened guy. Finn is the total opposite of *you*, Sam."

"Finn?" Sam cracked up. "That's his *name*? What's his last name, Huckleberry?" Sam doubled over in hysterical laughter. "Well, congratulations. But, um, I wouldn't be so sure you'll be having a *real* relationship. Serious, ambitious, intelligent, and what was that last one—oh, yes, *enlightened* med students don't do anything but study and take advantage of their oh-so-impressive status with every girl on campus."

"Oh, like you know?" Elizabeth snarled.

"I know *guys*, Elizabeth. Hope you like sharing."

"You know what, Sam? Let's make a deal. You stay out of my love life, I'll stay out of yours." She headed for the stairs, happy to at least have gotten the last word.

"Finn." She heard him laugh before he turned up the volume.

*　　　*　　　*

Todd turned the key in the front door of his apartment as quietly as he could. Dana was a light sleeper.

He pushed open the door, surprised that the lights were on. What was Dana doing up at—he glanced at his watch—4:45 A.M.?

She was sitting on the sofa, her textbooks piled on the floor by her feet. Her cello lay right in the center of the throw rug. But she didn't look like she'd been studying or practicing. She was wearing a red teddy. And she looked pissed. Very pissed.

"*Three*, Todd?" she questioned in a strained voice. "It's almost *five*."

"I know, Dana, I'm really sorry," he said, sitting down next to her. "I went out after work with Ryan—I told you about him, the DJ? And all of a sudden, it was like four o'clock. But Dana, I had the biggest blast! Ryan is the coolest guy—you would love him. He wants to become a record producer and open up his business, and you should hear how up he is on the industry; it's amazing and—"

"Todd," Dana interrupted, "you said we'd talk when you got home. And there's a lot we have to talk about. You blew me off."

"Dana," he said, taking both her hands in his. "I didn't blow you off. I would never do that—you know that." He looked into her eyes, but she was angry. Being sweet and mushy wasn't going to get him anywhere. "I figured you'd be exhausted or

135

asleep at three anyway, so how could we really talk about stuff? That's the only reason I didn't come home after work. And you know how it is when you start working somewhere. You want to get to know your coworkers, hang out with them—"

"Maybe your *coworkers* don't live with their girlfriends, Todd. Maybe no one cares if they don't come home when they say they will."

"Dana, come on," he said, trying to stifle a yawn, which he knew would be the ultimate insult to her. She'd think he wasn't taking her seriously. And he *was,* but he was just so tired. All he wanted was to hit the sheets. He had to get up at eight to make his management class by nine.

"Were you studying? Practicing?" he asked, gesturing at the books and her cello and hoping to change the subject.

"No," she replied. "I brought everything in here to take stock, I guess. Just look at everything and think, you know?"

What? What was she talking about? "Take stock? Of what?" he asked, getting up to stretch.

"Todd, I've been trying to talk to you about this for a week," she said, and he heard the impatience in her voice. "About school, how bad things are." She looked down at her hands, as if she were about to cry. He sat back down and sighed. Maybe too loudly.

"Look, Todd," she snapped. "If you're not interested in my problems, just say so, okay? I mean, you're making it clear anyway, so why am I even trying?" She started to get up, but Todd gently pressed her shoulders back down. She slumped on the sofa and put her face in her hands.

"Dana, Dana, sweetheart, listen," he said, taking her hands away from her face and holding on to them. "I *am* interested. Of course I'm interested. I love you. Dana? Will you look at me? Please?" She turned to face him, and he could tell her anger had been replaced by hurt.

What was he supposed to do? Say? He didn't want to have some long conversation about how everyone in her music classes was better than she was, how she didn't feel like she belonged at SVU anymore, how she just wanted to be with him. He wanted the Dana she'd been right before school started.

"I know you're having a rough time in school right now," he told her, "but you're just adjusting, that's all. We've both got a lot going right now. Adjusting to living together and taking care of our own apartment, and—"

"God, it's like you're not even listening." She shook her head. "I'm not talking about 'not adjusting.' I'm talking about not having *it* anymore. It's like I've lost every shred of talent I ever had. I used to be the *best*, Todd. The *best*. And now I

137

can't even keep up. I don't know what happened and—" Dana put her face in her hands again.

She looked up at him. "It's not about practicing more or harder; don't you understand? It's like I'm just not meant to be focusing on school right now. I think that's it. I think that's why I'm so off in playing and why the thought of spending an hour and a half in English lit or biology drains my blood. Does that make any sense?"

She stared up him expectantly, waiting for him to say, "Yes, baby, it does; I totally understand what you're growing through; why don't you just be a house girlfriend for the semester and focus on making the best macaroni and cheese you can?" Was that what he was supposed to say?

"But Dana," he started, and then shut his mouth. Anything he said would be wrong. He wished he could tell her she just needed to get psyched about something again, and then she'd be all right. The way he was about Frankie's now. Todd wasn't exactly Mr. College either; it wasn't like he loved school or had anything to say to the idiot frat guys in his classes anymore. He was an adult who had his own apartment and lived with his girlfriend and was starting to pay his own bills with his own money. He wasn't into hanging out in the student center or coffee shop with friends, checking out girls, and talking about the "great party, man."

But he was *supposed* to be in school. He didn't have to love it; he didn't have to get A's. He just had to show up, pass, and have a good time with Dana and at work. Why wasn't Dana understanding that that's the way it *was*?

Maybe that was it. Yeah. She just needed a *new thing*, like he had Frankie's. She needed something else other than him. That's why things were getting so strained between them—because she was expecting him to be that other thing too.

"Dana, I think I understand," he told her, feeling a new burst of energy. "I know exactly what you need!" He could hardly believe he'd figured it all out—at five in the morning, no less.

She sighed with relief and resettled herself on the couch, her legs tucked under her. The tears glistening in her hazel eyes cleared up a little.

"You just need a new thing, Dana!" he told her. "That's all!"

"A new thing?" she repeated. "What are you talking about?"

"You know, like Frankie's for me. Something that'll psych you up again, something you can get excited about so you can get through the drudgery of school."

"Todd," she began, uncrossing her legs and placing her hands on either side of her hips. "I don't want to *get through* the drudgery of school.

Cello *was* school for me. It was *everything*. I'm a music major, Todd. You don't *get through* cello."

"Well, you've got to get through *somehow*, Dana," he snapped, suddenly feeling very tired again. He always said the wrong thing with her lately. Always. "Because I need to get some sleep."

"Maybe if you'd come home when you said, it wouldn't be five that we're having this conversation." She got up and kicked her textbooks out of her way. "Hope the sofa's comfortable for that sleep you need. I guess I wasted wearing this," she added, gesturing at her silky red teddy before slamming the bedroom door.

Chapter
Eight

"Since when do *you* use a curling iron?" Jessica asked Elizabeth as they stood in front of the mirror in the bathroom between Jessica's and Neil's rooms. Jessica dug through her giant basket of hair supplies and handed it over. Elizabeth even using a blow-dryer was news.

"I just want to see what my hair looks like with the ends angled under," Elizabeth replied, staring at her hair in the mirror.

Tell her, Jessica thought. *Tell her about Tristan. This is the perfect time. You're dying to tell someone.* But then again, there wasn't much to tell. She'd gone for her second tutoring session, and it was exactly like the first had been. She'd impressed herself and him with that "eye" he kept talking about, but he hadn't flirted, hadn't looked deeply into her eyes, hadn't done anything—except excite her about art and frustrate her about his lack of interest in her! And now their tutoring sessions were done. But Jessica wasn't about to give up. That's what visits during office hours were made for.

Jessica stared at Elizabeth's reflection. She still wasn't sure she should tell Elizabeth. She knew she'd get that "so that's why you're so interested in art all of a sudden" response. And that wasn't true. The more Jessica read her textbook, the more she studied paintings, the more excited she became about what she was learning. Tristan was added inspiration. That he loved a subject that was becoming so important to her added something she'd never experienced before with a guy she liked.

Elizabeth was peering into Jessica's makeup basket. She watched Elizabeth pick up a lipstick, uncap it, then choose another. "Oh, so on this exciting Thursday morning," Jessica said, "before what, your journalism seminar, you suddenly want new hair and lips?" Jessica clicked open her compact. She saw Elizabeth flush just slightly. "Ohmigod!" Jessica exclaimed, turning to face Elizabeth and grabbing her wrist. "Give it up, Liz. Who is he?"

Elizabeth smiled and sat down on the rim of the bathtub. "I have a date tomorrow night with the guy of my dreams!"

"What? When? Who is he? Why didn't you tell me?" Elizabeth had a date with her dream man, and Jessica couldn't even interest Tristan!

"Well, I would have told you before," Elizabeth said. "But I haven't seen much of you this past week. I've seen *way* too much of Sam, though."

"I know—the guy is a total pig," Jessica complained, whisking her blush brush across her cheek. "And do you believe he ate the last of my Cap'n Crunch?"

"Blame your friend Chloe too," Elizabeth said, rolling her eyes. "I saw her stuffing a dry fistful of it into her mouth yesterday afternoon."

Jessica frowned. "Chloe? What do you mean? She was here yesterday?"

"Jess, Chloe was here all last weekend, half of Monday, practically all of Tuesday night, and most of yesterday afternoon. She's always hanging out with Sam. I told you last week I was worried about them."

Wow, Jessica thought. She hadn't even realized Chloe had been around. Between going to the library to look through art books, hanging out at Theta house, and walking around daydreaming about Tristan, Jessica hadn't been in the duplex much at all.

"Are they fooling around?" Jessica asked. "She doesn't seem like Sam's type. *You* seem like Sam's type, you know? I mean, not his type-type, but if he was going to actually date someone longer than one night, I'd think he'd go for someone like you. It *was* you he went for last summer."

"What do you mean, someone like *me?*" Elizabeth asked. "And please, don't remind me about last summer." Jessica knew that Elizabeth had really liked Sam. That they'd shared more than a few not-so-innocent, amazing kisses.

"You know, on his level," Jessica explained. "Someone really smart, not some flaky type. Not that Chloe's flaky—she's just *young*."

"You think Sam is *smart?*" Elizabeth asked in disbelief. "The guy who watches wrestling and plays video games and builds pyramids of beer cans in the living room?"

"You know what I mean, Elizabeth—you know Sam," she said. "Smart. Like, worldly. Sam might be a lazy slacker, but he's got this other side to him. The two of you are on the same wavelength deep down."

Elizabeth's mouth dropped open, and she stared at Jessica's reflection. "Wow, Jess," Elizabeth said. "Talk about having another side. That was pretty insightful."

Jessica beamed, and for a second she was overcome with love for her sister. She suddenly felt bad that they never spent any time together, never really hung out. Elizabeth's opinion meant more to Jessica than anyone's. And when Elizabeth acknowledged that Jessica was changing—as her sister was doing right now—becoming more mature, taking things more seriously, becoming *insightful,* it was as if Jessica had been given a gold star.

"Wait a minute," Jessica said, grabbing her mascara and edging closer to the mirror. "Who cares about Sam? Tell me about your guy!"

"Remember when I had to go to the ER last week?" Elizabeth began. "Because of so-smart Sam? Well, there was this med student observing the doctor who worked on me. Finn Robinson. Six-foot-two, blond, caramel-colored eyes. Gorgeous, Jess. I thought I'd made a total idiot of myself in front of him. And you should have seen me—hair in a ponytail, dirty SVU sweatshirt, ratty jeans, and he actually asked for my number!"

"Oh my God, he does sound gorgeous!" Jessica exclaimed. "So he called and asked you out?"

"And that's why I want to practice date hair today," Elizabeth replied, smiling and standing up to peer into the mirror. "Why does *your* hair look so good?"

"Liz, we have the same hair," Jessica said, laughing. "Although I might let you use the new extra-volume-enhancing shampoo I got—it's amazing and smells like green apples." Jessica grabbed the shampoo from the shower, uncapped it, and stuck it under Elizabeth's nose.

"Yum!" Elizabeth exclaimed. "That does smell great." Elizabeth capped it and stuffed it in her bathrobe pocket. If Elizabeth Wakefield was getting excited about volume-enhancing shampoo and practicing date hair, this Finn of hers wasn't just some regular cute guy.

"I've never seen you get like this about a guy, gorgeous or not," Jessica said. "He must have made a major impression on you."

"He's a *med* student, Jess," Elizabeth reminded her. "First year. That means he's older, more mature, sophisticated, knows what he wants to do with his life. Wait till you see him tomorrow night when he picks me up. He is so good-looking!"

Jessica smiled, but she couldn't help feeling a sting of jealousy. How had Elizabeth managed to get her med student to ask her out, looking all ratty and bloody at the ER, when Jessica couldn't get her grad student to ask her out when she worked on looking amazing?

Maybe green-apple shampoo wasn't the answer and Elizabeth had the real solution without knowing it. Still, Jessica didn't want to tell Elizabeth about Tristan, not yet. Not and ruin how impressed Elizabeth was with her.

"Isn't this wild, Jess?" Elizabeth said. "Me, all into a guy, and you carrying around heavy art textbooks and spending time in the library and getting tutored." Jessica had mentioned that she was getting tutored in art history because she liked how serious it made her seem. She just hadn't mentioned that her TA tutor was as gorgeous and amazing as Elizabeth's med student sounded. "It's like we've switched identities or something!"

"Scary, huh?" Jessica agreed, laughing. "So where's Dr. Love taking you?"

"A new Cajun place," Elizabeth said. "Isn't that cool? First date with an older guy and I'm already experiencing something new just by where he's taking me!"

"I can't wait to meet him," Jessica said, again feeling a little stab of envy. She wanted to be experiencing Cajun food with Tristan. Experiencing anything with Tristan. "Ooh—but I might not be around tomorrow night when he picks you up—I have a Theta meeting on rush week, and I have to be there."

"Don't worry about it," Elizabeth told her. "Hopefully he'll ask me out again, and you'll be able to meet him before any of our next hundred dates!"

Jessica beamed her biggest smile at Elizabeth, wanting to show her sister how happy she was for her despite her envy. Elizabeth deserved a great new exciting guy. Especially after wasting all of her dateable life on Todd Wilkins and Tom Watts, two of the most boring guys at SVU. Then again, even they'd changed, Jessica realized. Todd was living somewhere off campus with that cello player, and

Tom was the biggest deal on campus now that he'd rejoined the football team. It was like *everyone* was changing.

"I'm gonna go take a shower and try your shampoo," Elizabeth said, the excitement in her aqua eyes adorable. "Thanks, Jess," she added, and darted upstairs.

Jessica leaned closer to the mirror. Should she try the ponytail-and-sweatshirt look that had won over a med student? Would that snare Tristan when two attempts alone in his office and her all hottied up in discussion sessions hadn't?

She smoothed her hair, slicked on some lip gloss, and checked out her tight jeans and feminine shirt in the full-length mirror.

Change into a ponytail and sweatshirt? No way. Jessica had gotten something much more valuable just now from her sister: *inspiration*.

"Zippo, Alejandro!" Jessica complained, stirring a packet of sugar into her cappuccino. "Tristan's just not interested. I must be doing something wrong."

Alejandro found that very hard to believe. But what he couldn't believe even more was that he wasn't dead yet. Because listening to the girl of his dreams talk about how much she wanted Tristan Patterson was killing him. It had been ever since she'd asked him to get coffee with her after the discussion session. He knew she wasn't interested in *him* romantically; she was interested in more of his brilliant advice—about Tristan Patterson.

"I thought I might go up to him after class today and ask about another tutoring session," Jessica went on, "but he ran out of there so fast that I didn't have a chance."

"Chloe did too, I noticed. Maybe they're having some big affair," he joked.

"Chloe's too busy trying to have an affair with one of my housemates," Jessica said. "I think that's where she probably booked off to. Everyone's hooking up with who they want except for me!"

And me, Alejandro thought, staring wistfully into Jessica's blue-green eyes. God, she was beautiful.

"Twice, Alejandro," Jessica said, holding up two fingers. "I've been to his office twice this week. And he's had four times to see me in discussion session and ask to speak to me after. And he hasn't. So is he just not interested?"

Why did Alejandro have to be good at this? He knew *exactly* why Tristan Patterson wasn't going after Jessica. But if he told her, she'd know exactly what to do. And then Tristan and Jessica would probably start dating, and Alejandro would have to listen to how great their hot romance was. Which would make him sick.

Alejandro lifted his jumbo coffee cup in front of his face to give him time to think. He liked Jessica too much not to be straight with her, but did he have to deliver her into another guy's arms?

"What's wrong with me, Alejandro?" she asked. "Tell me. I totally trust your opinion."

Alejandro sighed. "Jess, there's nothing wrong with you." Maybe she'd just give up and then finally notice the guy sitting right next to her.

"Then why?" she asked, her shoulders slumping. "At first I thought he might have a serious girlfriend or something, but I don't think so. I can tell from the way he looks at me that he's interested. It's like he *wants* to ask me out but *won't*."

She ripped off a piece of his cinnamon bun and popped it into her mouth. He was mesmerized by her shiny pink lips moving.

Maybe he was wrong about his theory of why Tristan wasn't asking her out. After all, if Jessica was so sure she could tell that Tristan was interested in her, why couldn't she tell how interested in her he himself was? Maybe Tristan *wasn't* attracted to Jessica. *Yeah, right.* What guy wouldn't be? Alejandro had to be right about his theory. It was the only thing that made sense.

"Just out of curiosity, Jessica—how exactly can you tell?" he asked. Maybe she did know that he was sitting here dying to kiss her. Maybe she just wasn't acknowledging it, hoping his crush would go away.

"Lots of ways," she said. "Sometimes there's a certain way he looks at me. Other times I can tell by little things he says or does. Believe me, Alejandro, it's obvious to a girl when a guy likes her."

Alejandro almost laughed. Maybe he just hid it well.

"I am so frustrated," she said, wrapping her hands around her mug. "You've got to help me out here. What can I do? You're so amazing at giving advice. And you're a guy, so you know how guys' minds work."

She was staring at him so beseechingly that Alejandro's heart softened. He wanted her to be happy, wanted her to have everything she wanted. Even if it wasn't him.

He drained his coffee. "Jessica, Tristan's our TA, right?"

"Right . . . "

"So that means being the teaching assistant is his *job*," Alejandro pointed out. "He's obviously not asking you out because of professional ethics."

"Ohmigod!" Jessica exclaimed. "I never even thought of that! Professional ethics, of course!"

He waited.

"I know exactly what to do!" She breathed a deep sigh of relief. "Alejandro, you're brilliant! Absolutely brilliant." She leaned over and kissed him on the cheek, then dug into the rest of the cinnamon bun.

His heart sank. But he'd done the right thing by telling her his great theory.

"All I have to do is ask *him* out!" Jessica said. "As long as *he's* not doing the asking, it's fine."

Alejandro put down his mug and turned to face her. "Jessica, I just realized something. It actually might not matter to him *who* does the asking. I mean, if he's such a good guy, like you say, he probably would *never* date a student. Maybe it's against policy for TAs to date students in their classes. That would make sense because of their influence with the professors and with grading exams. Wow, you know, that *is* really weird. Maybe you should just forget it." *And then notice me.*

"Oh, come on, Alejandro!" Jessica said. "*Policy?* I mean, I understand about grading exams and everything, but it can't be *against* policy for a TA and a student to date. It's probably just *frowned* upon, if anything."

"Yeah, *frowned upon* for a really good reason," Alejandro noted, suddenly queasy about the whole thing. The more he thought about it, the ickier it seemed for a TA to date a student in his class. "I mean, let's say Tristan was dating some girl in our section and she was getting straight A's on exams he graded when she was really failing. Is that fair?"

"Alejandro!" Jessica exclaimed. "I can't believe you'd think Tristan would do that. First you're telling me his professional ethics are keeping him from asking me out, and now you're saying he's capable of being *unethical*."

"Look, Jess, I don't know him, okay?" Alejandro said, feeling very weary. "I just know it's *weird*, that's all."

"Weird, but not *unethical*. Not if *I* ask *him* out. I'll make it perfectly clear to him that if I deserve an F on an exam, then I want an F. Wow, so I guess we'll have to keep it really hush-hush. I mean, if he even says yes."

Like Tristan would say no. *Please*. And that meant the guy deserved an F in his job. Why didn't Jessica understand that?

"Dana?" Todd called out in the tiny apartment. "Dana—you here?"

No response. *Good*, he thought. *That must mean she's on campus, probably on her way home from classes.*

The past week had been so strained and weird. Every time they'd try to talk, it ended in an argument or a slammed door and Dana saying he just didn't get it.

Well, he didn't get it.

He walked into the bedroom, startled to see Dana lying on the bed. She was crying. *Not again,* he complained inwardly. He didn't have the time or the energy or the patience anymore. He had only a half hour before he had to go to work, and he didn't want to spend it arguing or trying to comfort Dana when he didn't know how.

"Dana," he said, and she looked up at him. Even tear streaked, her face was so beautiful. He loved her so much, but he just didn't know what to do.

"Did you have another bad day?" he asked, peeling off his shirt and tossing it into the laundry basket. He opened the dresser and took out a navy blue T-shirt. "Dana?" he prodded, slipping the shirt over his head.

It was so weird. Just days ago he would have been over to the bed in a heartbeat, stroking her hair, holding her in his arms, his heart breaking with concern for her. But now . . .

"Todd, I've really tried taking your advice about school," she said, sitting up on the bed. "I've been going, I've been dealing, even in mixed-strings class and in my cello seminar. But it's the same thing every time. Either I forget the right textbook for a class or I screw up playing and I feel like everyone just stares at me and thinks I'm such an idiot."

Todd sat down on the edge of the bed. "Dana, I know it must feel like that, but you know how people are—they really don't care. You're doing fine; you really are."

"That girl, Becky, who I told you about?" Dana said. "Today she had the nerve to snap at me in class. *'Slower, Dana.'* God, I felt like punching her! And twice the professor stopped us because I *was* too slow. I hate him, I hate her, I hate everyone at school."

"Except me, I hope," he said, pulling her into his arms. "Maybe you can switch to another strings class?"

"It'll just be the same," she responded. "It's not them, Todd. It's *me*."

Todd looked into her hazel eyes and wished he knew what to say.

"And then I suddenly realize I have no one to talk to, you know?" she added, looking like she was about to cry. "I mean, aside from you. That's why you end up getting saddled with it. I have no friends, Todd. No one."

She was right, he realized. After her old housemates had kicked them out at the start of the semester, Dana had sworn she'd never speak to them again. And they were the only girlfriends Dana had had. She'd made a lot of enemies last year when she'd tried to come between Elizabeth and Tom.

Todd glanced at his watch. He had to go. "Dana, I wish I didn't have to leave, but I do—Rita asked me to come in early to help her go over some problems in the books. Isn't that great? She really thinks I've got a good head for business. You see—all these business classes I'm taking really matter."

"So now you're going in *early?*" Dana complained. "Todd, we hardly get to spend any time together as it is. Can't you tell her you'll work on the books *during* your shift?"

"I have to *work* during my shift, Dana," he snapped, and then regretted it. He knew she needed him to soothe her, but he *did* want to go to Frankie's early. He took pride in the fact that Rita had asked him to help her out, that she thought he was capable of it even though he was just a sophomore in college. Even *though* he was in college. No one else at Frankie's was in school, and they sort of looked down on college students, like students were all rich snobs in fraternities and sororities. That they thought he was a cool guy meant a lot to him.

Dana snaked her arms around his neck. "Don't be in such a hurry. You must have enough time for this," she whispered, drifting kisses down his neck.

"Dana, that feels so good," he murmured, kissing her cheek and trying to keep his impatience in check. "But I really have to go." He gently peeled her arms from his neck and backed away, then stood up.

She was looking at him as if he'd slapped her.

"Hey, I have a great idea," he said. "Why don't you come down to Frankie's later, like around nine or ten, when it's hopping? You'll see what a great place it is, and I can introduce you to my coworkers. Annie, one of the waitresses, is really into music too—she's amazing on piano, and you two would—"

He saw Dana wince. *I am such an idiot,* he thought. *Like Dana really wants to hear that one of the girls I work with is really into music too.*

"I have a lot of laundry to do tonight," she said. "And I'm not feeling too social anyway. Maybe tomorrow night. Tomorrow's Friday, so Frankie's will probably be really fun on a weekend night, right?"

He drew her into his arms and hugged her. "It's a date." Todd felt a little better. Once she got back into circulation, she'd probably get back to normal too.

"I do have ten minutes to spare," he whispered into her ear, pressing her down onto the bed.

Nose to nose, Dana opened her eyes and smiled. "I love you, Todd," she said.

"I love you too," he whispered, and pulled off her sweater.

Chapter Nine

"Tristan?" Jessica called, poking her head through the ajar door to his office. "It's me, Jessica Wakefield."

"Jessica! Hi," he said, pulling the door open. "How are things going?"

Things haven't *been going*, she wanted to say. But they were about to start. Now that it was Friday, there was no way she was letting a whole weekend go by without trying her best to make something happen between them.

She stared up at him, dumbstruck as usual by how good-looking he was, how warm his smile was. Sunlight from the window glinted in his hair, and the dark blue sweater he wore with his faded jeans made his eyes seems even bluer.

"Um, I'm really sorry to just barge in on you," she said, "but I thought if you had time, you could help me with something. A painting," she added.

He glanced at his watch. " I do have about twenty minutes right now," he told her. "Come on in."

Jessica sat down on the love seat and pulled her textbook out of her knapsack. "It's this one," she said, holding it up to him. "I just don't get my reaction to it. It's like I can't even understand why it's considered art."

Tristan looked at the picture and smiled.

"A six-year-old could have painted this," she told him. "Right?"

He laughed. "Jessica, you won't love or admire every piece of art. But art historians do need to *appreciate* the merit of each piece. Whether it's the style, the technique, the subject, whatever."

He sat down next to her. "Do you understand?" he asked.

"So, what you're saying is that even if someone's technique isn't so perfect, the *style* might make up for it?"

"Well, sometimes," he said, looking at the textbook. "And—"

Before she lost her nerve, she leaned over and kissed him on the lips, not too soft, not too hard, and she waited for his reaction.

"I see you understand my point perfectly," he whispered, deepening the kiss and pulling her even closer.

*   *   *

"But what I am supposed to do in the meantime?" Nina wailed at the housing officer. "My roommate is a total psycho! There has to be another room somewhere on this campus. It doesn't even have to be a single."

"I'm sorry, miss," the man told her, turning away from his computer screen to look sympathetically at her. "There's really nothing I can do but put your name on the waiting list. As I said, I'll notify you the moment a space becomes available."

Nina clenched her fists. "But you told me earlier this week that there would probably be a few openings now." The man shook his head. "There has to be someone who's willing to switch— maybe someone who hates her roommate?"

"I'll notify you," the man repeated, looking behind her at the next person on line. Nina's shoulders slumped. She'd avoided Shondra as best she could the past week. She'd thought the girl would calm down with time and go back to being seminormal, but Shondra was still acting like a psycho. Conducting purification ceremonies, casting spells, chanting in the middle of the night.

Nina left the office in utter defeat and walked back to her dorm. When she opened the common-room door, she wished she'd forced the housing officer to come see what she had to deal with.

161

Shondra was standing on a rickety stepladder, smearing black paint on the walls.

Nina closed her eyes and prayed that when she opened them, this would all be a dream. Make that a *nightmare*. She was so used to Shondra's bizarre ways that she was almost blasé about what she saw now.

"Nina!" Shondra backed off her ladder, slinging a trail of black splatters across the drop cloth on the floor. This was no dream. "I'm glad you're home early. I've already painted my room, and I'm almost finished in here. I thought I'd do your room next, but I didn't have a key."

"Shondra, why on earth would you think that I'd want my room painted black?" Nina stepped around a dripping paint pan. "This is hideous. And you're just going to have to repaint it white when the RA sees."

"Like the RA ever comes in our rooms. And anyway, we have to be allowed to express ourselves, Nina. This paint is symbolic of the pain we're feeling. In blackening these walls, we're surrounding ourselves with the darkness of our souls."

"Shondra, you really have to get over this guy and move on," Nina shouted. "I mean it. You're really scaring me. I got dumped too, and you don't see me wasting my life painting rooms black and casting love spells. Move *on*, Shondra."

"You're such a bitch, Nina," Shondra spat, then continued painting.

There wasn't even an adequate word to describe what *Shondra* was.

Nina *had* to move out. If only she'd accepted Elizabeth's offer to move into the duplex, she thought, mentally kicking herself for the hundredth time. Now the empty room had been taken. And Nina had nowhere to go.

Ohmigod, ohmigod, Elizabeth thought, staring at herself in the full-length mirror that hung on the inside of her closet door. *Finn's going to be here in five minutes, and I have nothing to wear!* She slipped out of the floral sheath and let it pool around her feet, then tossed it at the growing pile of discarded clothes on her bed. What was she going to do? She'd tried on everything in her closet, and nothing was right.

She pulled on shorts and a T-shirt and ran downstairs to Jessica's room to root through her sister's closet. "Perfect!" she announced, pulling out an ice blue tank dress with a matching cropped cardigan. Not too dressy, not too casual. And feminine.

She ran back upstairs and changed, then studied herself in the mirror. *Yes,* she thought. *This is just right.* She spritzed on her favorite perfume, brushed her hair again, put back on the lipstick she'd wiped off, and slipped on her black strappy sandals.

The doorbell rang. Suddenly her heart started racing. She couldn't believe how nervous she was.

The doorbell rang again. Elizabeth hurried downstairs, then took a deep breath and opened the door. There he was, all six feet plus of him, looking amazing. He wore a black blazer over black jeans, a white button-down shirt, and a cool tie.

"Wow," he said. "You look great."

She smiled. "That day we met wasn't one of my finest moments." She laughed, stepping out and locking the door behind her.

As he led her to his car, a black convertible, she smelled his cologne, spicy and intoxicating. He opened the passenger side for her and closed it when she was settled in the seat, then hurried around to his side and slid in.

"We're off," he said, turning the key in the ignition and smiling an incredible smile at her.

Yes, we are, she thought.

If I were an artist, I'd paint that setting sun, Jessica thought as she hurried across campus toward Theta house. The sky seemed to have more colors tonight than she'd ever seen. It shimmered with streaks of reds, pinks, and oranges and giant swirls of purples, grays, and blues.

The whole campus seemed alive with new colors tonight. The lawn and trees—had they always been this smooth and green? Had the stucco buildings always been so white? Had the Spanish-tile roofs been so red before she and Tristan had kissed for the first time, just an hour ago? Had the world ever been this beautiful before tonight?

She spread her arms and twirled dizzily, laughing as she recalled every wonderful word Tristan had said to her. She was so happy! Her breath quickened as she remembered the warmth of his lips against her skin.

I am so in love!

After that second amazing kiss they'd sneaked off campus in Tristan's SUV to a huge park. They'd found a secluded spot under a big tree and had kissed and kissed, but they'd also talked a lot, about each other and art too.

And when she'd asked him out, he'd accepted. A real date. Tomorrow. An official date to spend the whole day together. She hadn't brought up his being a TA and her being a student, and she hadn't asked why he hadn't made a move. If it was a sensitive topic, as Alejandro seemed to think, why ruin things by making an issue out of it?

All that mattered was that she'd gone for what she wanted—and he'd been receptive. She couldn't wait to tell Alejandro that his advice had been right-on again. At least about Jessica having to be the one to do the asking.

As she turned down Sorority Row, she could see the Thetas' massive brick Victorian house ahead. There were girls on the porch, girls out front on the lawn, and more girls coming down the sidewalk. Maybe she should ask Alejandro if he wanted her to fix him up with someone. There were so many cute girls in Theta.

After rush week, when she got to know the freshmen pledges, she'd find someone for him. Someone really perfect, just like Tristan was perfect for her.

What better way to thank him for bringing love into her life than to bring love into his?

Dana stepped out of her bubble bath and wrapped herself in a thick towel. She smelled like wildflowers. She slipped into the satin robe Todd had bought her last summer and smoothed moisturizer on her face, then started putting on her makeup.

This felt so good—getting ready for a night out. Her favorite song came on the radio, and Dana darted into the living room to turn up the volume. She boogied her way back into the bathroom, so in the mood to dance tonight. Her usual classical station was now turned to a dance channel.

She felt like a different person. Why? She didn't

really understand it. She could go out any night she wanted, so why was this such a big deal? *Maybe it's because you* haven't *gone out in weeks,* she realized. *You've been sitting around in your sweats, moping and crying and acting like a baby.* Just getting ready for a night out at Todd's club made her forget her problems.

And it wasn't like she really had problems—not anymore. If she wanted to take the semester off and figure out what was wrong with her ability to play cello or just take a break, period, she could. It was really that simple. She had Todd, and that was all she needed. And all she wanted. Making a nice home for them, partying with him at night—what else could she ask for? Maybe she'd even get a job at Frankie's.

She was *so* looking forward to going to Frankie's tonight and so glad that it had been Todd who suggested it. After all, he wouldn't have asked her to come down tonight if he hadn't wanted to be with her, right? Not only were she and Todd going to be together all evening, but she'd also finally meet all those people he'd been gushing nonstop about.

She danced over to the closet. *What am I going to wear?* Nothing she pawed through seemed right. "I know!" She pulled a suitcase from the bottom of their small, cramped closet and threw it across the bed. It was full of clothes she hadn't bothered to unpack because their apartment was so limited on space.

"Wow! I haven't worn these in forever." She dumped out a pile of funky retro party clothes. These clothes had once been her trademark, but she'd been trying to dress more maturely since she and Todd had been together. Her old wardrobe had seemed too silly for a person with serious commitments. But she'd forgotten what fun they were. That these clothes were her *style*. *You've lost yourself somewhere, Dana Upshaw—that's what's been wrong.*

She shook out a psychedelic-print minidress and slipped it on. *Now, what shoes?* "My water platforms!" She looked in the corner behind the bed and dragged out a heavy cardboard box. Digging through it, she finally found her funkiest shoes, the ones that went perfectly with that minidress.

She stepped into the shoes and danced back to the bathroom. Standing in front of the mirror, she studied her hair. Lately she'd been letting her hair dry naturally into long curls or just pulling it up into a bun. But tonight she turned on the blow-dryer and grabbed her big, round brush. Stick-straight hair would look perfect. And because she'd started getting ready so early, she had the time to spend on getting her hair really straight.

A half hour later she spritzed hair spray on her smooth, long hair and admired it in the mirror.

"Hello, Dana Upshaw. Long time, no see."

Todd was going to be so happy that the Dana he knew and loved was back. Maybe once he saw how happy she was now, he'd realize she was right to drop out for the semester. Dropping out was all she'd been able to think about all week, but she'd been too upset about it to realize it was the answer to her problems.

She turned off the radio and the lights, grabbed her tiny shoulder bag, and headed out, ready to have the time of her life.

Chapter
Ten

Elizabeth's eyes widened as Finn led her inside the Bayou Bay Grill. The place was wild! Every inch of the fun restaurant was decorated with fishing gear, upturned washtubs, carnival masks, fake alligators, lobsters, and shrimp. Mardi Gras beads dangled everywhere.

There was a long wait for tables, but Finn had made reservations, so they were seated immediately. *Robinson, party of two . . . right this way, please.* She loved being part of that party of two.

"Like it?" Finn asked as he opened his menu.

"I love it—it's so much fun!" Elizabeth looked around, then back at Finn, and she could tell she was beaming. She could actually feel herself glowing. Her first-date jitters had disappeared, thanks to the long drive here. She and Finn had talked so easily in his car, about SVU, what they were

171

studying, and their favorite places on campus. This was going to be the greatest date of her life—she could tell already.

"What I love so much about this place is that it reminds me of home," he told her, reaching out to tuck a tendril of her hair behind her ear.

The light touch of his finger against her cheek sent such a charge of electricity down her neck that Elizabeth almost jumped. If he could do this to her by just touching one strand of her hair, what would it feel like to kiss him? To feel his arms around her?

"Home?" she asked, trying not to stare at him. He was so good-looking, it was difficult to peel her gaze from him. "Didn't you say you were from California?"

"My other home." Finn took a sip of water. "Where I grew up as a kid. I didn't move to California until I was fifteen."

"New Orleans?" Elizabeth guessed, and he nodded. *Cool*, she thought—he was from somewhere far away and exotic. Every second he got more interesting! "You don't have an accent at all," she noted aloud. "My first roommate ever at SVU was from Louisiana—she had the sweetest-sounding drawl. But she was the meanest person I've ever met."

"I know the type well." He laughed. "My drawl comes out when I visit my dad—he still lives

172

there. My parents are divorced, so I split my time between both places."

He's so worldly, Elizabeth thought, just as the waiter arrived to take their order. She realized she hadn't even cracked open the menu. "You know what?" she told him, slapping her hand on top of the menu. "Totally surprise me. Order me whatever you think a Cajun novice should try."

"Adventurous," he said, giving her an "I'm impressed" look. "I like that."

Finn ordered a couple of appetizers (she had no idea what they were or even how to pronounce them) and blackened catfish for her and seafood jambalaya for himself. She loved the sound of everything!

A waitress walked by with a steaming bucket of little red creatures that looked like a cross between baby lobsters and mutated shrimp.

"What's that?" Elizabeth asked, suddenly nervous about what was going to appear on her plate.

"That Cajun delicacy is known by many names. Crayfish . . . crawfish . . . crawdads, and my personal favorite, *mud bugs.*" He smiled at her. "I didn't order that for us—I figured I'd save that for the next time we come here."

The next time. That meant he planned to ask her out again! She was so happy, she'd eat an entire bucket of mud bugs.

* * *

The minute Dana saw the bright orange footsteps painted on the sidewalk, she knew Frankie's entrance was just around the corner. She couldn't wait for Todd to see her all decked out for him!

A group of people walked in, and Dana followed them. They looked a little older than she was, maybe early twenties. But they also looked more sophisticated—they definitely weren't college students.

Wow! she thought, looking around the small nightclub. Now she understood why Todd loved this place so much. It was so cool! Around the dance floor, explosions of light caught the crowd in surreal snapshots of color and action. Music pulsated around her. She could feel the bass pounding through her body.

As soon as her eyes adjusted to the darkness, she scanned the gyrating crowd for Todd. She didn't see him. Maybe he was working at the far end of the bar? People were standing three deep between the bar and the tables, so Dana had to weave her way through the dance floor.

Ducking around a woman who was dancing with a drink in one hand and a cigarette in the other, Dana almost got elbowed by a girl who seemed to be vibrating. She'd hardly gone three feet before a guy with numerous body piercings grabbed her and started dancing in front of her. She laughed and danced beside him a moment, then moved on.

This place is so much fun! She bumped and jostled and danced her way farther through the crowd. She was almost to the far edge of the dance floor when she finally spotted Todd. She paused, just to admire him from afar.

He looked so sexy in his T-shirt, faded jeans, and boots. His muscles bulged as he set a heavy rack of clean glasses behind the bar. She couldn't wait to surprise him. She planned to quietly get behind him, then tap him on the shoulder as if she needed to ask where the phone was or something. The look on his face would be priceless!

Suddenly the bartender working the far end, a blonde who Dana assumed was the Cathy she'd heard so much about, slid her arm around Todd's shoulders and whispered something in his ear. Todd laughed at whatever she'd said, then whispered something back.

That's Cathy? Todd had described the woman as "sweet with a great personality." Usually that was male code for not too cute. But the bartender was very pretty. And since the top half of her was barely covered by a glittery halter top, Dana could see that she was very sexy.

Dana doubted that Todd hadn't noticed Cathy was built like a Playboy centerfold, but he'd chosen to omit that piece of information when he'd gushed on and on about how nice and sweet she was. *Could the woman be standing any closer to Todd?* Dana wondered as anger rose inside her. The song changed, and Cathy started dancing as she slid a drink across to someone. Then she slid her arms around Todd's neck and shimmied down his body. A bunch of people standing at the bar started whistling and clapping. The two of them began whispering again and laughing.

Tears blurred Dana's vision, but she'd seen enough anyway. She wasn't going to stand here and watch her boyfriend dirty dancing with Miss November. She spun around on her platform shoes and ran out.

"I have one more surprise for you," Finn announced, slapping a few bills on top of the check.

Elizabeth spooned up the last bite of her key lime pie and licked her lips. "Another surprise? If it's as great as dinner and dessert, I'm ready."

She smiled, gazing at him and wondering how she'd gotten so lucky. Unbelievably, it was all thanks to Sam and his stupid beer-can collection that she was sitting across from this amazing guy. She'd loved everything he'd ordered (though the catfish was so spicy, she'd had to gulp water every few bites!). They'd talked nonstop during the entire meal, and twice he'd reached over and squeezed her hand.

"I'm taking you on a little boat ride in the Louisiana Bayou," he told her. "Right out back."

Her mouth dropped open. "A boat ride? Out back? Are you kidding?"

"Nope," he said, smiling. "There's a garden behind this restaurant, with a path that winds through magnolia trees and oak trees dripping with Spanish moss. And right in the center there's a bayou—well, maybe more like a big pond. And there are rowboats and paddleboats—it's so great. Shall we, *chère?*" he prompted, taking her hand.

No one could be this romantic, Elizabeth thought. Everything about Finn Robinson was like a dream come true.

Her hand tingled in his. He led her to the rear of the restaurant, then suddenly stopped short at the door to the garden. Elizabeth looked around him to see a beautiful girl blocking their path.

"Well, well, so *this* is why you haven't called," the girl said. She looked Elizabeth up and down, then narrowed her eyes on Finn.

"Stephanie," he said uncomfortably. "Um, this is Elizabeth—she's also a student at SVU."

"Like I *care* who she is. You have a lot of nerve, Finn. Dumping me without a word of explanation and then showing up at *our* favorite restaurant with this . . . this . . . *girl* practically before I have time to erase your message off my machine."

Elizabeth tried to retreat a step, but Finn slipped his arm back around her and held her tightly.

"You are the biggest liar and the biggest jerk," Stephanie hissed.

"Stephanie, look, I'm really sorry, but—"

"I'd be careful with him if I were you," Stephanie snapped at Elizabeth, then stormed past them into the restaurant, crashing into Finn's shoulder. Finn looked at Elizabeth, and she could tell he was embarrassed. Without a word, he pushed open the door and escorted her outside.

Finn took both her hands in his and pulled her over to a white wrought-iron bench at the edge of Bayou Bay's swamp garden. "Elizabeth, I'm really mortified," he said. "I'm so sorry about that. She didn't take the breakup well, and I guess it was hard for her to see me with another girl. I'm really sorry you had to deal with it."

Elizabeth touched his arm. "Finn, it's okay, really," she said. "Breakups are hard, and some-times they're messy. I'm not defending her or any-thing, but she's obviously not over you."

An ex who couldn't let go was something Elizabeth understood all too well. It had taken Tom half the spring and all summer to finally ac-cept that it was over between them. But what had

Elizabeth rattled was that for a second there, she thought Finn was two-timing Stephanie with her. And now she wondered if he was dating other girls. She knew she had no right to ask, not on a first date, but she hated the idea that Finn might be seeing other girls.

"But I'm way over her," Finn said, "and I don't mean to sound like a jerk. It's just that she turned out not to be the nicest person in the world, which you just got some evidence of."

Elizabeth nodded, and Finn pulled her to her feet. "Please don't tell me that episode ruined the rest of our night," he said, looking into her eyes. "That would kill me, Elizabeth."

It would kill her too. "I think someone promised me a moonlit boat ride in a bayou."

Chapter Eleven

Sam heard two car doors slam, then footsteps, then the jangling of keys. He fluffed up the pillow under his head, stretched his cramped legs over the edge of the sofa, and shoved the biology textbook he'd been reading for the past hour under the 49ers blanket that covered him. He scooped up his Spanish 2 and American literature books from the coffee table and shoved them under the blanket too, along with the highlighter he'd swiped from Elizabeth's room. Then he switched off Neil's hula lamp and turned on the television, flipping the channels until he found a horror movie.

And then he waited.

He could hear hushed voices outside the front door. He strained to listen. Yup, it was them. Elizabeth and Dr. Cool. Her heard her laughter, then a guy's voice, then silence. A few minutes later she jiggled her key in the lock. Sam figured the silence was the good-night kiss.

"So how was your date with Dr. Cool?" he called out when she opened the door. "Did he talk anatomy all night?"

"Do you *ever* leave that sofa, Sam?" she retorted. "Oh, I forgot! Clingy Chloe must be under that blanket somewhere."

"That's pretty witty for 2:30 A.M., Wakefield," he said. "So, seeing Huckleberry again?"

"What do you care?" she asked.

"Just curious," he replied. Why *did* he care? he wondered suddenly. He was never going to hook up with Elizabeth Wakefield again, that was clear. Even if he wanted to, which he didn't, she'd slam the door in his face. He'd never be serious, ambitious, or enlightened enough for Lizzie. But care he did, for some reason.

"Not that it's any of your business, Sam, but yes, he told me he'd call. So I *will* be seeing him again."

"Ah, the famous *I'll call.*" Sam muted the television with the remote. "I wouldn't wait by the phone if I were you." Any guy who said, "I'll call," rarely did. If you liked the girl and wanted to see her again, you asked her out right then and there. Why girls didn't get that was beyond him.

"No, Sam, I think it's only *you* who's famous for the *I'll call,*" she shot back. "Finn's a gentleman. And by the way, your jealousy of him is showing again."

"I couldn't be jealous of anyone named Finn." Sam unmuted the television.

"You're *so* mature, Sam," Elizabeth said, heading toward the stairs. "If Chloe's under that pile of blankets, tell her good night for me."

"That's twice you brought up my sweet, innocent freshman, Lizzie," Sam pointed out. "So let's not throw around words like *jealous.*"

"I am *not* jealous of Chloe," Elizabeth insisted. *"Please."*

"Well, *I'm* jealous of people who are *sleeping!*" Neil shouted from atop the stairs. "Could you both shut up already?"

"Sorry, buddy," Sam called, and a door slammed.

"Great, now you woke Neil up," Elizabeth accused. "You're so thoughtless, Sam."

"Oh, *I* woke him up," he snapped. "I'm not the one traipsing in at 2:30 A.M."

"No, *you're* the one who's sitting in the living room, waiting up for me at 2:30 A.M."

Sam stiffened, and he noticed that she did too. "You *were* waiting up for me, weren't you?" she announced, narrowing her eyes at him. "Why?"

"You're the one who keeps pointing out that I never leave this sofa," he reminded her. "I wasn't waiting up for anyone. I'm just where I always am, Wakefield."

"Whatever," she said, and took the stairs two at a time.

But he *had* been waiting up for her. *Why* was a question even smart-aleck him couldn't answer or didn't want to think about. He turned off the TV, then snatched up his pillow and blanket and headed for his room behind the kitchen.

The way he felt about Elizabeth was one of life's great mysteries. One way too deep to try to figure out at 3 A.M.

Todd crawled into bed beside Dana, set the alarm clock, and stretched out. Man, he was beat. But it was worth it. Frankie's had done amazing business tonight, and his share of the tips had almost shocked him. He'd had no idea he could make such good money by having so much fun.

He looked over at Dana's sleeping form. He was worried about her, big time. That she hadn't shown up at Frankie's tonight meant she'd probably had another bad day at school. But that was getting as tired as he was right now. He felt justified in being so pissed off at her for blowing him off tonight. He'd told everyone his girlfriend was coming to hang out and meet them, and all night they'd asked him where she was. That she was a no-show had embarrassed him—it made him look bad, like his own girlfriend had better things to do than see where he worked and meet his friends on a Friday night.

Suddenly Dana shot up in bed, startling Todd. "Okay, I'm just going to come right out and ask you this, Todd, and I want you to be honest."

He stared at her. "Are you seeing Cathy?" she asked, looking him dead in the eye. "I want the truth."

"Seeing Cathy?" he repeated. "The bartender at work? What do you mean, *seeing her?*"

"I mean, I saw the two of you tonight at Frankie's," she said between gritted teeth. "She was dancing her Playboy-bunny body up and down against you—or didn't you notice?"

"You were there tonight?" he asked, stunned.

"*Hel-lo?* You *invited* me to come, Todd." She threw her pillow across the room. "I got all dressed up—I was so psyched—and I find you and the bartender all over each other, whispering and laughing. I got the hell out of there real fast. I guess I did you a favor because if I'd stayed and thrown up on the floor, you'd be the one who'd have to clean it up—"

"I can't even believe this," he interrupted. "You see me and the bartender, my coworker, for God's sake, dancing by the bar, and you assume I'm cheating on you? I *invite* you, but then I'm stupid enough to be all over some girl? Give me a break."

He was so angry, he got up and paced to the

window. "I told everyone you'd be coming. I couldn't wait to show you off. I felt like such a loser when you didn't show up."

He paced back to the bed and stared at her. "You really think I'd cheat on you, Dana?"

She looked down and scrunched the edge of their comforter in her hand. She lifted her gaze back to him, staring at him for a few seconds. Then her expression changed, from anger to something more like frustration. "I just don't know, Todd," she said. "But it looked bad. If you'd seen me and some guy like that, you'd have done the same thing. Actually, you would have probably beat the hell out of the guy."

"Dana," Todd said, kneeling down by the edge of the bed. "I'm going to tell you this for the last time. I love you. *You*. I'm not seeing anyone, I'm not cheating on you—I'd *never* cheat on you. I'd never want to. Cathy's an extrovert, that's all. There is nothing going on between me and her, and I don't want there to be."

She seemed to be considering that for a few seconds, but then she jumped out of the bed and into his arms. "I'm sorry, Todd," she said between sobs. "I'm really sorry. I know you wouldn't. I feel like such an idiot."

Todd sighed and held Dana, wondering what the hell had happened to his relationship. The

186

relationship that had been so strong, so great.

He knew what had happened, though. *Dana had changed.* Maybe it was partly his fault for suggesting they move in together. Maybe it was all too much, too soon.

"Well," she said with a sniff, "at least tomorrow is Saturday. We'll have the whole day together before you go to work. Just you and me."

"Dana, I wish I could, but I really have to hit the books tomorrow, for at least a few hours." He felt her stiffen. "Sweetie, you know I don't get to study much during the week because of work. If I don't spend a good chunk of tomorrow in the library, I'll be in big trouble. I have an economics exam on Tuesday, and I haven't even cracked open the book."

"Fine, forget it, I understand," she said, and hopped back on the bed. She pulled the covers up and turned away from him.

Todd sighed. It was pretty bad when studying seemed like a better time than Dana.

Chapter Twelve

The second Jessica woke up, her excitement overwhelmed her and she bounded out of bed. Today was her date with Tristan! It was already almost eleven, and she was supposed to meet him in the parking lot behind the arts building at one. That didn't give her much time.

She grabbed her robe and poked her head into the hallway. The duplex was dead quiet. It was no surprise that all her housemates were still sleeping, given how late they'd been up.

Jessica had been woken up in the middle of the night by Neil yelling at Sam and Elizabeth to shut up. Just when she'd fallen back asleep, she'd heard Elizabeth slam her bedroom door upstairs. Jessica hoped that wasn't an indication of how Elizabeth's date had gone.

She thought about going upstairs for details

before hitting the shower, but Jessica decided against it. Elizabeth probably needed the sleep. Anyway, they could swap date stories later tonight. Now that she and Tristan were officially dating, Jessica felt she could finally tell Elizabeth about him without ruining her new reputation as a serious student.

Once Jessica explained to Elizabeth what Tristan was like, how he inspired her, gave her confidence, made her feel she could do and be anything, Elizabeth would understand that he was a complement to her new studious ways—not the sole reason for them.

She dashed down the hall and into the shower. As she lathered up with her green-apple shampoo, she finally understood that saying about feeling like today was the first day of the rest of your life.

A huge smile spread across Elizabeth's face as she slowly drifted awake. She could still feel the imprint of Finn's lips on hers as he'd kissed her good night outside the duplex.

She'd never forget their first kiss—in the little rowboat on the fake bayou. After that one little kiss, she'd forgotten all about his irate ex or whatever that girl had been to him. All that mattered was the future—their future.

He'd rowed her around for about an hour, and

then they'd walked along the garden, hand in hand. When he'd brought her home, he'd gently held her face between his hands and kissed her so deeply and passionately, she thought she'd melt right there.

And then she'd come inside to find Sam waiting up for her. Waiting up to give her a hard time, to make fun of Finn's name, and to act like an all-around jerk. What was his problem? Why would a slacker like Sam, who never exerted himself for anything, spend so much energy tormenting her? Whenever she thought she had Sam figured out, he'd zap her, surprise her, make her wonder. Truth be told, she didn't know if it really was jealousy that was motivating him to be so sarcastic about Finn. If Sam *wanted* to be more ambitious, he certainly had the brains and the ability. So why, then?

Why are you even wasting your time thinking about it? she asked herself, kicking off her blanket and stretching luxuriously as Finn's perfect face came into her mind. She knew he'd call like he said he would. Sam didn't know anything about having a real relationship, and she wasn't going to let his opinion deflate her. Elizabeth recalled the way Finn had mentioned "next time" in reference to trying a delicacy at the restaurant. He'd made it more than clear then, in the bayou, and with that incredible kiss good night that he wanted to see her again. He'd call.

Smiling again, she got out of bed and noticed a piece of notebook paper under her bedroom door, half in and half out. In Jessica's loopy scrawl was: *Liz, took the Jeep, hope you didn't need it today, but I have a very hot date, I'll tell you about it later, can't wait to hear about your night! Jess.*

A very hot date? With who? Elizabeth wondered. And why hadn't Jessica mentioned it before, when Elizabeth had told her about Finn? Whenever Jessica didn't mention a *very hot date* in advance, it meant something was either weird, fishy, or troublesome about either the guy or the situation.

Give Jess some credit, she told herself, hearing Neil's voice inside her head. Her sister had changed a lot since school started, and maybe Jessica was just keeping quiet about her personal life as part of her new campaign to take things more seriously. It would be so cool if they both had great new boyfriends at the same time. Maybe for once their boyfriends would even get along, and they could double-date.

Elizabeth grinned at the thought and grabbed her laundry basket. From the lack of sounds in the house, it was clear no one was home. What a relief that she wouldn't have to deal with Sam's sarcasm.

She headed downstairs into the silent living room, surprised to see Sam sitting on the floor with his back to her. He sat cross-legged near the boom box, his head bent over something. A textbook, she saw. And he was wearing earphones. He was tapping his pencil to some beat on the page as he read.

Well, well. Not only was Sam Burgess *studying*, but he was actually being considerate by using earphones to listen to his eardrum-popping music.

Because he figured she was still sleeping after getting in so late and being kept up even later by him? Or because . . . Elizabeth couldn't even think of an "or because." Not once since he'd moved in had Sam ever listened to music with earphones. But why would Sam suddenly turn nice?

Unnoticed by him, she padded down the steep, narrow steps to the basement, which contained the boiler, a bunch of fat wires, the washer and dryer, the housemates' collective junk, and suitcases. She loaded the washer and headed back upstairs.

Sam still sat in the same position, tapping away on the pages of his textbook. Elizabeth went into the kitchen and stopped short at the sight of the dishes piled up in the sink and the bread crumbs all over the table. Neil was a bigger neat freak than Elizabeth, so this wasn't his doing. Jessica, maybe. But Elizabeth was sure all those dishes and pans were Sam's. She was about to storm into the living room and yank the earphones from his head to yell at him, but she decided against it.

Sam had done his first nice thing for her, so she'd let this one go. But just this one.

Awesome, Jessica thought, craning her neck back to take in the towering sculpture that dominated the lobby of the opulent Newman-Wallford Gallery. The sculpture must have stood three stories high, and the ceiling rose another two stories above it. Jessica had never heard of the gallery until today, until Tristan had brought her here, but the place was very well known and crowded with people dressed to the nines.

She could hardly believe she was in a Los Angeles art gallery *and* with Tristan Patterson. She slipped her arm around his, and he smiled at her, then leaned in for a kiss. "I'd better stop," he said, "or some of these people will think we're performance art." He laughed. "You could drop a tissue on the floor and wait ten seconds, and a crowd would come over and analyze its artistic merits."

Jessica laughed and squeezed his hand. Tristan was so amazing. He knew so much about art, and yet he was down-to-earth, not pretentious at all. He took her hand and entwined her fingers with his. They slowly meandered through the gallery, stopping to look at everything that caught their eye.

A tuxedo-clad waiter walked by with a tray of champagne, and Tristan snagged two glasses. "I have a little surprise for you," he told her.

Tristan took a few sips of his champagne, then set the glass on a window ledge lined with empty and half-full ones. Jessica did the same, and then he took her hand and led her up a wide marble staircase. Each riser was so short, it seemed to take a hundred steps to reach the top. He escorted her to a wall covered with a huge modern oil painting—violent slashes of different colors.

"What do you think of it?" he asked.

Jessica shrugged. "I don't know. It seems angry, like the artist was either really pissed off or maybe conflicted about something."

He laughed, and she felt her cheeks redden. "Are you making fun of me?" she asked in a joking voice, hoping she wasn't making a fool of herself.

"Of course not," he said with a smile. "You've just articulated exactly what this painting expresses to me. When I painted it, I was going through a rough time with my dad—we hadn't been getting along at all."

"*You*? You painted this?" She stared at Tristan, then back at the painting, and finally located his name scrawled in black, below a streak of gray in the lower-right corner. "Why didn't you tell me you had a painting here?"

"I wanted to surprise you," he told her, lifting her hand to his lips.

"It's incredible." A funny feeling came over her as she looked at the painting. The artist, the person who'd actually painted this, was not only standing right next to her, he was dating her! The reality was almost overwhelming.

"One day I hope my paintings will hang in my own gallery," he said.

Jessica was surprised. "Don't you want to be a teacher?" she asked

"A teacher? No, not at all," he replied. "Being a TA helps with my graduate tuition, that's all. I like the job, but teaching isn't my passion. Art itself is, and painting."

"Tristan Patterson in the flesh," a male voice exclaimed from behind them. Jessica whirled around to see a very attractive guy around Tristan's age smiling at them.

Tristan extended his hand, and the other man shook it. "Jessica, this is a good buddy of mine, Joseph Wallford. We were both fine-art majors together a few years ago. Joe, Jessica Wakefield."

Jessica's eyes widened. "Wallford? Like the gallery?" she asked. "This is yours?" She swept out her arms.

"More like my family's," he replied. "I see you've been checking out Tristan's work. Talented guy. I wish he'd forget getting a master's in art history and go back to painting. I'd display all his work."

Jessica's mouth dropped open. She stood staring at Tristan, in total awe, as he and his friend caught up. She'd had no idea Tristan was so connected.

For the next two hours Jessica had an incredible time, moving from exhibit to exhibit, listening to Tristan's deep, sexy voice as he talked about the piece or the artist or just about art in general. Every once in a while he'd lift her hand to his lips and kiss her fingers or her palm. As they left the gallery, Jessica's head was spinning—overcrowded with a million new facts and ideas about the world of art . . . and with the knowledge that she was in love.

He took her to a huge outdoor restaurant that overlooked the Pacific, where they feasted on salmon, and then to an adorable beach town for the "best chocolate-chip cookies he'd ever had." By the time they pulled into the parking lot behind the arts building, it was 9 P.M. The only other car left in the lot was Jessica's Jeep.

The thought of going their separate ways filled her with a sharp pang. She wouldn't even mind just sitting here in his car, with the console between them and everything. She could sit here with him for hours and be happy.

"I have a great idea!" She beamed a smile at him. "Let's go dancing! Do you know Starlights? It's just a couple of blocks from here—it's the greatest club and—"

"Um, Jessica," he interrupted, "We can't—" He turned away from her, staring out the side window.

Had she said something wrong? Done something wrong?

"Tristan? We can't what? I don't understand."

He turned back to face her. "Jess, I would love nothing more than to go dancing with you. "Especially *slow* dancing." He smiled and trailed his finger across her cheek, down her throat, and over to her bare arm. "But Starlights is a little too close for comfort, if you understand what I mean. . . . "

She had no idea what he was talking about. Too close for comfort? Huh?

She was dying to take him to Starlights so that all her friends could check him out and—*Oh.*

Now she understood. Starlights was way too close to *campus* for comfort. That's what he'd meant. If everyone saw them together, especially with their inability to keep their hands and lips off each other, there'd be hot gossip about the TA seeing the student in one of his discussion sessions.

"I guess we have to be discreet, huh?" She suddenly remembered Alejandro's warning that things would get complicated.

"Very," he replied. "It's definitely not cool for me to be dating you while you're in my discussion section. I could get fired, maybe even get kicked out of the program."

"So *that's* why you asked me to meet you here," she said as things started making sense to her, "instead of picking me up at my house. Took me all the way to LA for our date. That's why we hunted around for that very secluded spot in the park yesterday."

"I thought you understood all this, Jess. I'm sorry."

"I did, I guess," she told him. "But I didn't think beyond having to keep it quiet. It never occurred to me that we'd have to actually hide that we were seeing each other."

Which meant that not only couldn't she parade Tristan up and down the halls of the Theta house, she couldn't even tell her friends about him. Thank God she'd been discreet enough not to have done that already. All Lila, Denise, and Alexandra knew was that she'd met a grad student and was hoping he'd ask her out. And Alejandro knew everything, of course, but she totally trusted him.

Tristan sighed. "I know it's not fair to you, Jessica. I really want to be with you, but I'll understand if this is just too complicated and you don't want to see me again."

"I *do* want to see you again—and again and again," she whispered, touching his arm. "I'm just ashamed that I didn't realize how dangerous this was for you." She leaned back in her seat. "Does this mean we can't go anywhere ever?"

"Of course not," he said. "Didn't we go

everywhere today? We just can't hang out on campus or too near it."

Jessica considered her options. Give him up, or keep him secret.

It was no contest. Being with Tristan was the important thing. Besides, she had always been drawn to the forbidden. Keeping her relationship with Tristan a secret might be exciting. "It won't be so bad," she told him. "We'll just have to be careful."

He reached for her, and she tried to slip into his arms, but the console made an embrace practically impossible. "I guess this means we have to shake hands, say good night, jump into our own cars, and go home now."

It wasn't like they could go to his place since he lived in faculty housing on campus. And the duplex was off-limits since it was full of SVU students, even if one was her own sister and the other two were friends.

She sighed. "I wish I'd known this earlier. I would have kissed you more before." She reached for the door handle.

Tristan grabbed her arm. "We could always go to my office and snuggle up on the love seat for more of those kisses, Jessica," he suggested. "It's not the most romantic place in the world, but it's private."

A private rendezvous at night in Tristan's office? He had no idea just how romantic that was to her.

Chapter Thirteen

"Oh, uh, hi, Liz."

Elizabeth looked up from her newspaper and glass of orange juice, surprised to finally see her sister's face. *Oh, uh, hi, Liz?* Something *was* wrong. And Elizabeth was sure it had something to do with that "very hot date" Jessica had scribbled the note about on Saturday.

Jessica had said, "Oh, uh, hi, Liz," as though she hadn't expected her sister to be in the kitchen and wouldn't have come in if she'd known. And now Jessica seemed to be avoiding looking at Elizabeth. Her twin had made herself scarce yesterday, which all but shouted to Elizabeth that something was up.

"Hi, stranger," Elizabeth said, deciding to force the issue. "I've been dying to ask about your date."

201

"Date? What date?" Jessica ducked her head into the refrigerator and rooted around for something.

"What *date?*" Elizabeth asked, staring at her. "The *hot* date you needed the Jeep for on Saturday? The *hot* date that kept you out all day and half the night? You left me a note, remember?"

"Oh, *that* date," Jessica said, shutting the door. "You know, I'm really not that hungry—," she added, turning to leave.

"Jessica," Elizabeth said, standing up and grabbing her sister's wrist. "What's going on?"

"Nothing. Really." Jessica wriggled out of Elizabeth's grasp and filled a glass with tap water. "It was a hot date with, um, the Thetas—I've been over at Theta house practically all weekend to plan for rush."

Elizabeth looked Jessica in the eye, which was difficult since her sister was looking everywhere but at Elizabeth. Fine. If Jessica didn't want to talk about her date, Elizabeth wasn't going to prod or pressure her. Elizabeth only hoped Jessica wasn't in some sort of mess.

"So, do you mind if I take the Jeep today?" Jessica asked. "I know it's your turn, but I really need it."

"Jess, you had it all weekend," Elizabeth pointed out. "And I need it today—"

"What time are you leaving?"

"In like two minutes," Elizabeth said, glancing at her watch as she spooned up the last bite of cereal. "I'm meeting Nina at the coffee shop for breakfast."

"Can I ride to campus with you?" Jessica asked. "I need to do something before my art-history class."

"Of course you can," Elizabeth replied, truly worrying now. Since when did Jessica Wakefield ask if she could *do* anything? Elizabeth washed her glass and stacked it on the drainer. Jessica sprinted out of the kitchen. Something was up with her sister, Elizabeth knew. Something Jessica definitely wasn't ready to talk about.

Though only seven hours had passed since she'd last seen Tristan, Jessica couldn't wait to feast her eyes on his gorgeous face, feel his arms around her, hear his voice. They'd spent most of yesterday together, a perfect Sunday, talking, kissing, laughing, sharing their hopes and dreams. They'd used his office again last night as their secret place. And although there was something exciting about having to keep their relationship a secret, Jessica hated that she couldn't tell everyone about it.

And she hated that she'd lied to Elizabeth

earlier at the duplex about the date on Saturday and where she'd been yesterday. As her sister pulled the Jeep into the commuter parking lot, she gave Jessica that look—the look Jessica knew meant "I can tell something's wrong." Jessica thanked Elizabeth for the ride, adding a silent thanks for not demanding answers.

Jessica hurried to the arts building. She had only fifteen precious minutes to spend with him before class started. His office door was wide open. Tristan was sitting at his desk, bent over a stack of papers with a look of intense concentration on his face. She glanced to the left and to the right in the hallway—the coast was clear. With a smile she slipped inside and closed the door.

"No one saw you come in?" Tristan asked, looking behind her nervously.

"Nope, I checked." She came around the desk to sit on his lap.

"Jess, we can't," he said, shooing her back around the desk. "Devane doesn't always knock— he could just barge in. Can you imagine if he found you sitting on my lap?"

"Okay, okay." She sat in the leather chair facing his desk.

He gazed into her eyes. "All right, c'mere, you," he relented, leaning forward to kiss her over the desk. "I've missed you, Jess—isn't that crazy? I just saw you, what? Less than eight hours ago, and I've been sitting here, missing you."

"Me too," she whispered as her heart flip-flopped. "I'll be thinking so much about you that I won't be able to concentrate in lecture. I wish you were teaching that class. Devane's so serious and stuffy."

"But he's an excellent professor and knows his stuff inside and out," Tristan said. He glanced at his watch. "And speaking of Devane, you'd better get going, or you'll be late."

He stood up and reached over the desk for a quick kiss. "I wish things were different, Jess. If they were, I'd stand in the middle of campus and scream out how I feel about you."

"I know," she whispered, touching his face. "I would too."

She got up and headed for the door, turning back for one last long look.

"Spiders—a jar full of them," Nina raged to Elizabeth, taking a sip of her cappuccino. "I thought painting the rooms black was bad—now I have to worry that one of her spell-casting spiders will crawl out of that jar and—" Nina felt the tiny prick of tears at the backs of her eyes. "I don't know what to do."

"Nina, why didn't you tell me any of this was

going on?" Elizabeth asked. "I've been leaving messages for you for over a week, and you never called me back." Elizabeth looked hurt. "I thought we vowed just two weeks ago to be there for each other. To turn to each other for support."

"I know, Liz," Nina said. "But—"

"No buts, Nina," Elizabeth cut in. "We're best friends."

Nina didn't know how to explain why she hadn't called without sounding pathetic. But Elizabeth was right. They were best friends, and Elizabeth was the only person she could tell anything to without worrying about being judged for it.

"I know what it's like to have the roommate from hell," Elizabeth said. "*Housemate* from hell." She held up her hand, and Nina could see a dark line of stitches. "Sam's precious beer-can collection— I fell right on top of the open end of the tab." Nina looked down at her cappuccino, and Elizabeth rushed to continue, "Not that Sam's a psycho like Shondra, but Nina, you could have told me. I mean, maybe I could have thought of something to help."

"I'd trade Shondra for Sam in a second," Nina said. "Slob or not."

"Hey, maybe Shondra can put a spell on Sam," Elizabeth said with a smile. "Get him to actually wash a dish, buy his own food, and turn down his stereo!"

Nina laughed. Talking to Elizabeth and venting did make her feel better, but Elizabeth would be going home to a great off-campus house that she shared with her own sister and two friends. And Elizabeth even had a new guy in her life, a med student. Nina had a nightmare living situation, no guy, no social life, and a ton of studying to do.

Nina would gladly welcome Elizabeth's problems with Jeep-hogging Jessica, Mr. Neutral Neil, and Sloppy Sam. They all sounded pretty great to her.

"I wish I'd taken you up on your offer to move into that fourth room when it was available," Nina said. "I would have saved you the headache of Sam and myself freaky Shondra." She threw her napkin on the table.

"Ohmigod!" Elizabeth shouted. "Nina, I just thought of something!"

"I'll listen to anything at this point," Nina replied.

Elizabeth scooted her tray to one side and leaned across the table. "Our house has a finished basement. It's not that big, and the washer and dryer are down there, but the rest of the space is just full of our junk. If we cleaned it out, you could move down there—it would make a perfectly good bedroom!"

Nina actually felt her heart lift. "Do you think Jess and the guys would be okay with it?" She was afraid to get too excited.

"Are you kidding?" Elizabeth asked with a laugh. "A fifth roommate would break the rent even more—Neil would be thrilled! I'd be thrilled just to have you around. Sam won't even notice, and Jessica would be fine with it. Definitely no problem, Nina!"

"Great!" Nina said, a huge smile on her face. "All I have to do is pack. My stuff and I will be there in a few days."

Alejandro turned around to check the lecture hall's entrance again. *Finally,* he thought as Jessica hurried into the auditorium. After not laying eyes on her all weekend, he was dying to see her.

"Jessica!" he called, waving her toward the empty seat next to him. He'd moved to the last row so that he could snag her as she came in.

She dropped into the aisle seat beside him. "Thanks for saving me a seat." She leaned over and hugged him.

She smelled like wildflowers and vanilla and looked absolutely ravishing. She was glowing, he realized. *Because she hooked up with Patterson?*

Alejandro looked at his watch. "I was afraid you weren't going to show up today. You know what kind of notes *I* take."

"I'd never blow off lecture." She smiled a dreamy smile. "I was with Tristan—in his office."

Alejandro gritted his teeth. "*With* him?" he repeated, not wanting to hear the sordid details. Had Patterson caved and made his move?

"I can't wait to tell you everything!" she exclaimed. "I took your advice and asked him out, and he said yes! Tristan and I spent all of Saturday together and then Sunday too. It's totally top secret—we have to be really careful that no one sees us together. It's so exciting and—why are you looking at me so strangely?" She tilted her head to one side and studied him. "Alejandro? What's wrong?"

Alejandro felt his stomach churn. Tristan Patterson was a class-A jerk. The man had no right to be leading on a student. Maybe Patterson really did like Jessica and have strong feelings for her, but Alejandro would bet anything the guy was just fooling around, when Jessica was taking this very seriously. And as a TA, Patterson shouldn't be dating his student. Alejandro was sure the guy was breaking policy.

The whole thing made him sick. As did the fact that it was partially his own fault. He should have thought it through before he'd ever suggested she go to Patterson for tutoring.

"Oh, uh, it's nothing," he lied. "I was just thinking something. Sorry. So, top secret, huh? That must be a real drag."

"Well, sort of." Jessica smiled. "But Tristan makes it so exciting. We go far off campus, and then when we get back, since we can't bear to be apart, we just go to his office and snuggle up on his love seat! I can't wait to run downstairs to his office after class—Alejandro, you're giving me that weird look again. Is something wrong?"

"Um, uh—" Alejandro frantically tilted his head a few times toward the door behind her, but Jessica wasn't getting it. *Dr. Devane* was standing in the doorway, just a foot away from where Jessica sat. The professor was staring at Jessica's back, and he looked furious. It was clear he'd heard every word of Jessica's exciting affair with Tristan Patterson.

Devane, Alejandro mouthed, jabbing his finger toward the door.

"What, Alejandro?" Jessica was staring at him as though he'd had grown another head. "What are you—"

"Miss Wakefield, is it?" grumbled the familiar voice of Dr. Devane.

Jessica whirled around. And then she whirled

back around to Alejandro, her suddenly pale face in a panicked expression. "Dr. Devane," she said, turning to him. "I didn't realize you were standing there."

"A word outside, please, Miss Wakefield." Devane gestured toward the hallway.

"Uh, sure." Jessica looked at Alejandro as she slowly got up.

Uh-oh. This was not good. If Jessica got in any sort of trouble over this, Alejandro would personally rip apart that bastard Patterson. If he could, that was.

As Jessica exited the auditorium, Dr. Devane instructed his lecture TA to dim the lights and start the slide projector and commentary. "I may be a while," he announced.

Idiot, idiot, idiot! Jessica yelled at herself. How could she have been so careless? Hadn't Tristan told her how important it was that they be careful, discreet?

And what had she done? Blabbed their relationship to Alejandro right in front of the professor! The large lecture hall was so packed with a hundred gabbing students that Jessica had thought no one could hear her. Who would have thought Devane would possibly overhear enough of anything to actually stop and listen?

The professor motioned for her to follow him into a small, empty classroom.

"Sit down, Miss Wakefield," he instructed.

Jessica perched on the edge of a chair and gnawed at a fingernail. She realized how guilty and nervous that made her look, and she dropped her hand to her side.

Dr. Devane paced back and forth in front of her. He cleared his throat. "Miss Wakefield, it has come to my attention that—"

He paused and stopped pacing. "Tristan Patterson is currently under investigation for the sexual harassment of female undergrads in his discussion sections, and—"

The blood drained from Jessica's face, and her mouth dropped open. She stared unblinking at Dr. Devane. "Tristan Patterson? You must be mistaken—"

"I'm afraid I'm *not* mistaken, Miss Wakefield." He looked her straight in the eye. "The students who were allegedly propositioned by Mr. Patterson strongly felt that their grades and test scores depended on accommodating him. Do you understand what I'm saying here?"

Propositioning female undergrads . . . accommodating him . . .

"Dr. Devane," Jessica began, trying to keep her voice even. "With all due respect, I absolutely don't believe a word of it. It's not true. It has to be some kind of big lie or something. Tristan, um, I mean, Mr. Patterson never propositioned *me*. And he had opportunity—he was tutoring me."

"As Mr. Patterson is well aware of the investigation into the alleged misconduct—"

What? Tristan *knew* about this? Jessica wondered, unable to wrap her mind around this entire conversation. Was *that* why he hadn't propositioned *her?*

No, wait a minute. This was *Tristan* they were talking about. Tristan, who she'd spent the most wonderful week of her life with. The guy who made her feel smart and special. Who made her feel beautiful and wanted. There *had* to be some mistake. There had to be.

"There will be a hearing, of course," Dr. Devane continued. "Several girls will be testifying—"

Jessica's mouth dropped open again. *Several* girls? She'd figured Devane was referring to two girls at most. Two undergrads who had fallen for Tristan and then spun a web of lies about him when he'd turned them down. But *several girls?*

"The young ladies will be testifying before the disciplinary committee," the professor added.

"Dr. Devane," Jessica said slowly. "How many girls is several, to be exact?" She had to know.

"Six," he said.

Six. Jessica sank back against her chair. Six girls making up the same story? That sounded as far-fetched as the charges being leveled against him. "What will happen to Tristan?" she asked.

"If the committee finds him guilty of the charges, he'll lose his teaching assistantship, of course," the professor explained. "And he very well might be expelled from the university. Miss Wakefield, the reason I bring this to your attention is that based on what I overheard, your testimony will be very important to the committee."

My testimony? What is he talking about?

"Why would I have to testify?" she asked, stunned. "I already told you—Tristan *never* propositioned me. In fact, I asked *him* out. I'll testify to *that*."

"May I call you Jessica?" he asked, sitting down in the seat next to her. Jessica nodded. "Jessica, listen to me. I understand your point, and I also strongly sympathize with your feelings. However, and please, think about this—six students have come forward to accuse Tristan of sexual harassment during the past two semesters. I wonder how many others were too scared to do that."

Dr. Devane took a deep breath. "I want you to think about a girl who might not be as strong-willed

214

or as confident as you are, Jessica. Think about that girl, most likely a freshman, away from home for the first time, worried about fitting in, making friends, having a boyfriend. And suddenly the handsome graduate student teaching one of her courses starts flirting with her. . . . She's flattered perhaps, but he seems a little too out of her league; he makes her nervous. Still, she's pressured to give in to his advances because of his influence on her grade. Jessica, do you understand?"

Tears sprang up in Jessica's eyes. She did understand. But there was no way she could reconcile the sickening graduate student who could do that with the Tristan she'd fallen in love with. Why would Tristan *proposition* anyone? He could have any girl he wanted.

"If you really believed these allegations, Dr. Devane," Jessica began, "why is he still allowed to be a TA? That lets him continue doing what he's accused of."

"If it were up to me, his teaching-assistant privileges would have been revoked and he'd be put on probation until the hearing. However, at this point we're simply conducting a pretrial investigation. He has not been formally charged with any wrongdoing. Therefore, he cannot be stripped of his teaching responsibilities."

"Well, I still don't understand why you'd want

me to testify." That made no sense. Anything she'd say would only weaken their supposed case against him, wouldn't it?

"Your testimony will illustrate that Tristan Patterson, even in the face of the investigation, is still carrying on with a student in his discussion section. A 'top secret'—to use your phrase—relationship."

Jessica's heart stopped for a second. She closed her eyes and sighed, then opened them when Dr. Devane continued. "Jessica, just imagine this: You end your relationship with Tristan, and he's angry. So he fails you on exams and papers and speaks negatively of your work in discussion sections to me. And I'd be none the wiser. So, let's then say you come to me and report the situation—if you're not too scared or embarrassed to, that is. But Tristan says you're lying, making it up—"

Jessica couldn't listen to another word. She shot up out of the seat. "I need to think this through, Dr. Devane. I—" She ran from the room and burst through the heavy double doors outside.

She ran as fast as she could, stopping behind a line of tall, heavy bushes that surrounded the library. Her knees gave out, and she sank down on the grass, her hands covering her face and drowning out the sobs that racked her entire body.

Chapter Fourteen

As Todd fished around in his pocket for change for the vending machine, the geek sitting next to him in the library gave him a dirty look. Todd ignored the geek and pulled out enough change for a candy bar and a bag of pretzels. A trip to the vending machine by the elevator meant a break from all this studying. He'd read his assigned chapters and then some for all his classes, and he was bored out of his mind. But he couldn't go home, and he didn't have to be at work for hours.

Couldn't go home. More like *didn't want* to go home, he realized as he stood up and stretched. Heading to the vending machine, Todd realized he'd again chosen studying over hanging out with Dana. After spending practically all of Saturday in the library, he didn't need to be here again today. And though he'd been studying over the weekend for an exam, today he was just killing time.

Because he didn't want to be with Dana.

Saturday night she'd felt guilty about accusing him of cheating on her with Cathy and ashamed that she'd pulled an attitude about his having to study. So instead of having a nice Sunday together, she'd spent half the morning crying. He'd spent half the afternoon reassuring her. And he was tired of it.

This wasn't the way it was supposed to be. He knew that having a relationship, a serious relationship, meant compromises—that it wasn't all fun and games. But he felt like all he *was* doing was compromising.

Todd dropped the change into the vending machine and pulled the knobs. He stuffed the candy bar in his pocket and ripped open the bag of pretzels, munching on his way back to his seat.

"Do you have to crunch so loud?" the geek asked as Todd sat down. "It's really distracting. And could you stop crinkling the bag?"

Todd stared at the short, scrawny guy, then realized he had to give the geek credit. Todd towered over him and probably weighted fifty pounds more, but the geek knew his rights and wanted them honored. When it came to studying, geeks didn't make compromises.

"Sorry," Todd said, collecting his books. "I'm leaving anyway."

He'd go to Ryan's; maybe shoot some hoops and hang out till their shift started.

Maybe he'd even ask Rita if she could use him tomorrow night—his night off.

Jessica paced back and forth in the American painters aisle of the library. An hour ago she'd left Tristan an urgent message to meet her here. Where was he? Had Dr. Devane gotten to him before she had a chance to talk to him? What was she going to do? She had a million questions and no answers.

Suddenly she saw him coming down the aisle toward her. "Jessica," he whispered. "What's wrong? What's the emergency?"

She stared at him, at the face she loved so much, at the guy who'd made her feel things she didn't even know she *could* feel. The accusations couldn't be true. They couldn't be. Tristan was crazy about her, wasn't he? He was a gorgeous, intelligent graduate student who had his paintings hung in galleries, for God's sake. No way was he going around propositioning students, pressuring them to—

She took a deep breath and leaned close to him. "I picked here to meet because it wouldn't look odd for us to be in this section of the library. If anyone comes, we can just pretend we're looking for a title," she told him.

"Jessica, tell me what's wrong," he whispered, staring at her.

"Dr. Devane knows about us." Jessica took a deep breath. "It's all my fault—he overheard me and—he wants me to testify against you, Tristan." Tears welled up in her eyes, and she blinked them away. "Tristan, tell me it's not true. I know it's not, but I need to hear you say it."

Tristan led Jessica farther down the row, looking behind him to make sure they were alone. He stared down at the floor, then looked back up at her. He pulled her into his arms and pressed his lips against her hair.

"Someone might see us," she whispered fiercely, shocked that he was being so open.

"I don't care anymore, Jessica," he said. "I tried to play by the rules, and it's gotten me in a mess of trouble that's not my fault."

"So it's not true!" she said, a smile breaking through. "I knew it!"

"Jess, I'm going to be really honest with you," he told her. "It *is* true that I was involved with those six students—"

What? What was he saying?

"Tristan, I—"

"Let me finish, please, Jess. Last year and during the summer session I did date those girls, two of them just once. But I didn't proposition *anyone*. They came to *me*. With each one I realized we weren't right for each other, so I ended it. Every one of those girls refused to take no for an answer—they were hurt and angry and—and suddenly I'm in a *lot* of trouble."

They came to him. Just like I did. "So, I'm just like any of those six girls," Jessica said, the tears stinging. "I thought I meant something to you." Jessica felt like the biggest fool on earth. As the reality seeped in bit by bit, Jessica leaned against the bookshelf for support and clapped her hand over her mouth. She felt sick.

"Jessica, no. *No.* Please don't believe that for a second." He grabbed her hands and held them to his chest. "I've been looking for you for so long. That's why I was dating so much, to find the woman of my dreams. *You.* You've got to believe that, Jess."

She stared at him. His expression was so serious and he sounded so sincere that she did believe him. She *wanted* to believe him. "We've talked some about my plans, what I really want to do with my life," he said. "I should be painting, maybe supporting myself by working in a gallery like the one we visited."

He tilted up her chin. "You won't have to testify or anything, Jess. I'm going to drop out of the program." He stared at the ground for a moment. "I'm sorry I didn't tell you about all this. I don't know if I was too embarrassed or if I was afraid you'd think I was a player or what. I'm sorry for everything."

So he was just going to walk away, she realized. Just leave, as if he hadn't hurt those girls . . . or her. As if he didn't have a responsibility to the discussion sections. To his own studies.

Even to her.

He's immature, she thought, stunned by the realization. *Even though he's older and more experienced.*

She wrapped her arms around herself. She'd gone from disbelief to rage to hurt in a matter of an hour, and now all she felt was sad and empty.

"I know this is confusing from where you stand," he whispered. "But if anything, please just know how much you mean to me. How much I wish we could have a real chance together."

"Oh, Tristan." She leaned against him, putting her hands flat on his chest. Suddenly it was all just too much. The truth, the lies, whatever. It didn't matter because he was making it not matter. He was walking away.

He held her so tightly, she could barely breathe. When he looked at her, she saw that he had tears in his eyes too. "I found what I was looking for you in you, Jessica." He kissed her wet cheek. "And maybe one day we'll find each other again."

She stared up at him. *Maybe. Or maybe not.*

"One last kiss, Tristan," she said. "That's what I want. Just one last kiss."

He pulled her into his arms and kissed her. She touched her lips and then gently traced his with her finger, taking one last look into those amazing blue eyes.

Then she turned and ran.

Chapter
Fifteen

"Sorry, Chlo, I can't," Sam said into the phone as he stretched out on the sofa. "I've got a ton of stuff I have to get done tonight."

Chloe let out a disappointed "oh," and Sam felt a little guilty. He actually was planning to do nothing tonight except listen to a new CD he'd bought and stare at the ceiling. But he'd been hanging out with Chloe a lot lately, and he wanted to cool things down, make it clear they weren't becoming a couple or anything.

He liked her a lot as a friend, but that was it. Sometimes he got the sense that was all she was into also, but then other times she'd flirt so obviously that he couldn't tell what she wanted from him.

"All right," Chloe said with a little pout in her voice. "I should hang out with my dorm-mates anyway—they're all totally pissed at me for never being around."

"Hey, Chloe, I gotta go," he lied. "I can smell my grilled cheese burning."

Guilt hit him again as he hung up. Chloe was such a good kid, and he didn't like lying to her. But better that he protected her.

The phone rang again, and Sam snatched up the receiver.

"Chloe, I really can't—," he began.

"Hello?" a male voice said. "I was looking for Elizabeth?"

Finn, Sam realized. That faintly southern "I'm-a-med-student" voice could only be Dr. Cool's.

"Elizabeth's not in at the moment," Sam told him. "Want to leave a message?"

"Finn, I'm tired of sitting over there by myself," Sam heard a throaty-voiced girl say. The sound of a palm slapped over the mouthpiece told Sam that Dr. Cool didn't want Elizabeth's housemate overhearing this little interruption.

"Would you let Elizabeth know that Finn called?" Dr. Cool asked.

"Finn," Sam repeated, just as Elizabeth walked in the door.

Finn? she mouthed at him, and Sam nodded. "Hey, um, she just came in, so hang on," Sam said into the phone.

He handed the cordless to Elizabeth and went into the kitchen. *What a jerk,* Sam thought. *The guy's actually calling Elizabeth when he's on another date.* How had Elizabeth managed to spend an entire evening with the guy and not see right through him?

"No, Thursday night sounds fine!" he heard Elizabeth say. "I can't wait." Silence. Small laugh. Silence. "Me too," she said. "Seven-thirty." Small laugh. "Bye."

Sam pushed back through the swinging kitchen door with a can of Coke and a ham sandwich. Elizabeth was staring out the bay window with a huge smile on her face.

"I'd be careful if I were you, Wakefield," Sam said, stretching back out on the couch. "I heard some girl in the background when he asked for you."

Elizabeth rolled her eyes. "I thought we agreed to stay out of each other's love lives, *Sam.* Hey, do you know where Jess and Neil are? I have the greatest news to tell you guys—house related."

"No clue," Sam said. He'd tried, which was all he could do. If Elizabeth wanted to get all hung up on a jerk, that was her problem. He was busy enough trying not to be one himself.

"Jessica!"

Jessica turned her head with zero enthusiasm

227

to see who was calling her. *Oh, thank God!* It was Alejandro. She'd been looking all over campus for him—she'd even stopped by his dorm.

He jogged over to her, his knapsack flopping on one shoulder and hers on the other. He was such a good guy. She'd forgotten all about her knapsack, which she'd left on the back of her chair in the lecture hall when Dr. Devane had called her out.

"Jessica, I've been looking all over for you." He grabbed her hand and led her over to a concrete bench. "What did Devane say? I've been freaking out—when you never came back to class, I got so worried." He settled their knapsacks between them on the bench.

Jessica was so overwhelmed with relief at having someone to talk to about this that she broke down. Tears streamed down her face, and Alejandro snaked his arm around her. She leaned her head against his shoulder, covering her face with her hands. She sobbed out the whole story, finishing with leaving Tristan in the library. "It's over," she said. "I'll never see him again."

The warmth of the sun and the weight of Alejandro's arm on her shoulders felt warm and comforting. Alejandro was the only person who knew about Tristan, the only person who knew the whole story now. One day she'd tell Elizabeth, but for now, she knew she was going to keep this one to herself. She had a feeling Alejandro wouldn't bring it up or even mention Tristan's name again.

"Thank you, Alejandro," she said, sitting up straight and taking a deep breath. She brushed away the wetness under her eyes and sniffed.

"For all the great advice?" he muttered.

"For being here for me now," she said. "For not saying 'I told you so.' You were right about . . . everything. But I did what I wanted to do, believed what I wanted to believe. Just like the old Jessica always did."

"Don't beat yourself up over this," he told her. "You didn't do anything wrong. You just followed your heart. Sometimes that'll get you what you want, and sometimes it won't. But at least you tried, Jess. You went for it. You know how many people *don't* go after what they want because they're too busy thinking of the reasons they shouldn't?"

"Yeah, but they don't end up with broken hearts either," she said.

"Because they never take risks. You had a great weekend with Tristan, right? Would you rather *not* have had it at all?"

"I hadn't really thought of it like that," she said, a small smile forming. "You're right—as usual. I'd rather have had that weekend than not have had it. Even if it means feeling this way right now."

Alejandro smiled and squeezed her hand tightly.

"You know what else?" she said. "Something really great came out of all this. I discovered how much I love studying art history. Yeah, I fell for Tristan, but I fell for art history too—big time. He really inspired me, Alejandro. Despite everything, I have him to thank for that."

"You have a really great attitude, Jessica," he said. "You'll find the right guy, I just know you will."

"Forget guys," she told him. "I'm just gonna focus on school and Theta right now—two things that are really important to me. I'll think about guys again once I'm more settled. I just hope Tristan *is* able to walk away as easily as he thinks he can—that there won't be a hearing. That way he'll be out of sight, out of mind."

Jessica saw Chloe walking up the path toward them. "Hey, there's Chloe." She waved, and Chloe ran over to them.

"What do you say the three of us hit the coffee shop," Jessica suggested. "I'm suddenly in the mood for their triple-decker ice cream sundae."

"Oh, good!" Chloe exclaimed as Jessica and

Alejandro stood up. "Because I really need your advice about guys, Jess. You too, Alejandro—especially because you *are* a guy. You know how guys think! It's Sam—he's just not interested, no matter what I do! Any suggestions?"

Jessica looked at Alejandro and cracked up with laughter. They each put an arm around Chloe's shoulders and headed for those sundaes.

Check out the **all-new....**

Sweet Valley Web site—

www.sweetvalley.com

New Features

Cool Prizes

The
ONLY
official
Web site!

Hot Links

And much more!

You'll always remember your first love.

Love Stories

Looking for signs he's ready to fall in love?

Want the guy's point of view?

Then you should check out *Love Stories*. Romantic stories that tell it like it is—why he doesn't call, how to ask him out, when to say good-bye.

Love Stories
Available wherever books are sold.